FIRST IN THE FIELD

A'ZEDI SURVEY CORPS
BOOK 2

BLAZE WARD

KNOTTED ROAD PRESS

First In The Field
A'Zedi Survey Corps: 2
Blaze Ward
Copyright © 2025 Blaze Ward
All rights reserved
Published by Knotted Road Press
www.KnottedRoadPress.com

ISBN: 978-1-64470-463-9
Cover Art:
ID 30150692 | Spaceship © Philcold | Dreamstime.com

Cover and interior design copyright © 2025 Knotted Road Press

Reviews
It's true. Reviews help. Even a short one, such as, "Loved it!" So please consider reviewing this book (and all of the ones you've read) on your favorite retailer site.

Never miss a release!
If you'd like to be notified of new releases, sign up for my newsletter.

http://www.blazeward.com/newsletter/

Buy More!
Did you know that you can buy directly from the Knotted Road Press website?

https://www.knottedroadpress.com/shop/

ALSO BY BLAZE WARD

The Science Officer Series

Start with: The Science Officer

The Jessica Keller Chronicles

Start with: Auberon

CS-405 (Command Centurion Kosnett, part of Jessica)

Start with: Queen Anne's Revenge

First Centurion Kosnett (sequel to Jessica)

Start with: Encounter at Vilahana

Additional Alexandria Station Stories

Alexandria Station Collection

Handsome Rob (Alexandria Station Universe)

Start with: Can't Shoot Straight Gang

=====================

Corsac Fox

Start with: Flight of the Corsac Fox

Operation Marrakesh

Start with: Trial by Leviathan

Captain Daring

Start with: Revoked

The Hunter Bureau

Start with: Mirrors

Fairchild

Start with: Fairchild

Last Stand

Start with: Lost Dreams

The Lazarus Alliance

Start with: Escape

Shadow of the Dominion

Start with: Longshot Hypothesis

Star Dragon

Start with: Birth of the Star Dragon

Kincaide's War

Start with: The Eden Package

Star Tribes

Start with: Winterstar

Blaze also writes Action-Adventure Here

CONTENTS

PART 1
JAFFRA'S CORNER

ONE

Maddox leaned against the tall table and enjoyed his beer. Mostly, because he had Squire Perry standing across from him, trying to pretend to be casual, while Serge Broom and Sankar Bachchan were dressed as miners, over in a corner.

Bar. Dive, really. World was Jaffra's Corner, which was a strange name for a planet, but nobody had asked him. Seen on a map, it had once—a very long time ago—been the anchor point off one of the major trade hubs, a side road turning off into the darkness of the *Unaffiliated* worlds generally coreward from *A'Zedi*, though they weren't all that far from any recognized *Wronlori* borders.

Still, far enough away from anyone that none of the usual governments had ever claimed the place. And the locals preferred it that way. Stubborn, opinionated, and fiercely independent. Like a lot of *Unaffiliated* worlds.

Stellar traffic was decent, but only one real city on the surface, and that was more of a town than anything. Felt rustic. Maybe fifteen thousand people within walking distance of this bar. Call it twenty kilometers.

Bar was a rough place, but that was as much reputation as anything. The day was only late morning, where the folks who had passed out and been stashed in a back room to sleep it off mostly had, while their replacements hadn't decided to come in and get serious about their drinking yet.

Wood bar, topped with stained and damaged copper sheet that hadn't been more than wiped in years, from the colors. No stools, so you stood to drink.

Maddox hadn't asked if there had been stools at one point, and they had all been broken in bar fights, or if the original owners had already known what kind of town this was and saved their money.

Lots of miners in a five-light-year sphere. A few farmers and ranchers here on the surface, mostly because they could work in peace and do their own thing.

And all the various and sundry folks that eventually collect to service and prey on miners if they sat still long enough. Bars. Restaurants with no aspirations to greatness. Dance halls. Saloons. Tap houses. Whore houses. Breweries.

And jails.

The *A'Zedi* Patrol Corvette *Kalyn Blackford*—aka "*Doctor Kay*"—was on a patrol run a little deeper towards the Core than usual this time. Survey Corps had gone ahead and forward-ported them out of Astarte III, but then had them clear the vicinity because Line Command was about to drop a small assault squadron on a pirate base Maddox and his crew had recently located, and Intelligence—who was his other boss—didn't want anyone connecting *Doctor Kay* with pirate busting.

At least not yet.

So he drank, in a dive bar with scarred walls, on a peaceful enough weekday morning, mostly sipping at a beer nasty enough to be used to clean industrial parts, but he supposed that miners and their ilk preferred it that way.

At least it was calm in here.

Until it wasn't.

Sudden noise had Maddox turning to look. Voices raised. Ugly voices. Ugly people giving vent to ugly emotions.

Perry, standing across the bolted-down table from him, ratcheted himself up a notch. Maddox didn't have to look to know that Broom and Bachchan would do the same.

He and Perry had worn their *A'Zedi* uniforms. Black pants. Mauve pullover. Mulberry jacket.

Doctor Kay had landed yesterday, so folks would be expecting to see him. Hopefully, Broom and Bachchan were mistaken for miners that had wandered in. Lots of small ships coming and going pretty regularly at the starport.

Flight Control Operations was about the only thing on this planet that folks appeared to take serious and professional.

"We don't like your kind around here," a man was snarling.

Him and several of his friends had someone backed into a corner. Smaller fellow. Fox, surrounded by wolves.

Odds didn't look good. Five against one.

Rest of the bar wasn't all that friendly, either. Most folks seemed willing to hunch down and pretend nothing was happening. Bartender had a hand out of sight, probably holding a weapon of some sort.

Maddox hoped that he wasn't about to be consumed in a brawl. He'd just gotten this uniform cleaned.

Fellow in the corner shifted his feet as Maddox watched. Maddox wasn't a close-quarters fighter like Perry and his two troopers, but he recognized someone preparing for violence.

A walking stick suddenly got reversed in the slender fellow's hands, and held like a sword in one hand.

Maddox had left the ship without any weapons beyond his three security troopers. He could see where that might have been an overambitious mistake on his part, assuming that Jaffa's World wouldn't be *that* dangerous.

In his defense, he *had* brought three killers with him.

"You need to go back where you belong," another rumbler announced in the mob.

They had their backs to him, so Maddox wasn't sure which one had spoken, but the others growled like pack hunters. Perry's hand vanished under the table. Broom and Bachchan tensed.

Maddox considered his options, but not for long, because one of the gang stepped in and threw a punch.

Might have been a pretty good brawler, at least in his own mind. Feet shuffled forward. Fist came up and lashed out like a snake's tongue.

Target wasn't there. Then the attacker went down with a hard crack. The other four rushed in.

Maddox turned to Perry, noting the anger in the man's eyes.

"You know, I'm not sure I like those odds, myself," Maddox said. "Feels unbalanced."

Perry rose to his full height. One hundred and ninety centimeters, though lean. Whipcord. Barbed wire. Ugly smile on the man's face.

"I got your flank," Maddox said.

He supposed that a Knight in Command of a Survey Corvette shouldn't get into brawls, but five on one—four on one now—didn't sound right.

And then it was nine on three, because several punks at the next table over decided to jump in as Perry went by.

Seven on three after Squire Perry did something with a fist

as the first punk got close. Too fast to follow, but the guy staggered backwards into a fellow, then both went down.

Maddox stepped into one of the others and punched him in the stomach as hard as he could, then sidestepped when the man doubled forward and started throwing up whatever was in his stomach besides beer.

Then Broom and Bachchan hit this group from the rear and it was suddenly over.

Maddox heard a gunshot fill the bar like a peal of thunder —who uses gunpowder in the modern age?—and the fox went down.

Maddox saw red. Simply charged the three still standing over there. Drove one of them into a second, then grabbed a hunk of iron that burned his hands as he twisted it out of the third man's control and head butted him in the nose because they were that close and he had his hands full.

Someone grabbed his arm, then changed their minds when Perry landed on their back. Broom and Bachchan landed a moment later, and Maddox realized that he and the bartender were the only two people still standing in here, a small group hunched down under table tops and his people thumping the ones that had started this mess.

Bartender started to snarl something and changed his mind when Maddox pointed the pistol at the man. Ingenious design. Intuitive, even, as his right hand wrapped around a grip and a finger found a hook he assumed was a trigger.

"No," Maddox snarled simply.

Man nodded and set a big stick carefully on the bar top before letting go and stepping back, probably pretty certain that any other response might get him shot, too.

A quick look around, but nobody else wanted to cause trouble at this moment, either.

"Perry, what's his status?" Maddox asked, not looking down.

Fists had stopped hitting flesh.

"He has a penetrating wound," Perry replied. "Bad but not necessarily lethal if treated quickly. I do not have the tools at hand."

Maddox found his comm with his other hand.

"Bridge, Deck Officer."

Armiger Narayana Yadav. Deck Officer of *Doctor Kay*. A man almost two decades Maddox's senior, but one who would never be promoted again, and it had apparently taken a lot of favors owed and a little blackmail by one of Yadav's former subordinates to get the man this far.

"Emergency protocol," Maddox said, invoking the highest alert. "Launch Boyce in *Packrat* soonest. Vector down on my radio signal and have her land in the street to pick up a wounded civilian for transport to the ship. Have Doc prepared for surgery."

If nothing else, Narayana was a stone professional. That had been one of the things that had saved him originally. He didn't ask. Didn't argue. Didn't anything.

Merely acted.

"Launching recovery soonest," he said, then cut the line.

Maddox nodded, noting the look of surprise on Perry's face.

Maddox handed him the pistol and squatted down next to the fox, where he got his second surprise today.

He was a she. Attractive woman, if not beautiful.

Bleeding, though.

"Bachchan, keep pressure on the wound," Maddox said, getting hands under the woman and lifting, still mostly powered by rage at this point, but it was a useful tool on days like this. "Broom, grab her gear. Perry, I want a perimeter enforced with lethal weapons if necessary."

Nothing Maddox had read about this world, or seen in the time he'd been here, suggested good Samaritans suddenly stepping up to help, and Maddox was pretty sure that the only medical training around here was probably a large animal vet, and he had one of those on the ship already. One he trusted.

Plus, most of the men on the ground at his feet had had some problem with the woman, so Maddox had to assume that she wouldn't be safe if left where the locals could get to her.

Woman was a lot more solid than she looked. Maddox staggered getting her upright, then followed Broom to the door and out into the street.

She wasn't going to die on his watch.

TWO

Narayana lifted the cover and rockered the alert switch, letting the siren wind up to wake the dead for several seconds before shutting it back down and opening the shipwide intercom.

"Boyce, launch *Packrat* immediately and located Knight Nevin in town by his comm signal," Narayana ordered. "Medical, stand by to treat a civilian casualty returning to the ship with the commander. Repeat, civilian casualty."

That last bit was probably necessary. Most of the crew still remembered Kumar Das, who had bent every rule and called in every favor he had in order to get Narayana back into space. Those same spacers had made life hell for the two commanders who had tried to replace Das, before Corps had given them Maddox.

And they'd since taken a cotton to the man, but Narayana had also reminded them how close they'd gotten to being broken up as a crew and blackballed on future assignments to the point that most of them would have had to leave service.

Even in the middle of a war.

Still, he found both his hands shaking and needed a moment to understand why.

Maddox Nevin reminded him too much of Kumar Das, and Kumar had gotten himself killed on a dumbass backworld like this, leaving Narayana with PTSD that had suddenly chosen to rise up and bite him.

He'd ask Doc Nordin for something later so he could sleep.

After the emergency settled.

Whatever the hell had happened today.

Squire Rolland Waters appeared at a dead run, buttoning his tunic as he slid to a halt, eyes wild. With the ship in harbor, even on dry land, and standing down for R&R and maintenance, Narayana had taken the full anchor watch himself.

Folks needed downtime. He'd carve out time for his own later.

After he knew Maddox was safe. Narayana could get this ship and crew home by himself if something happened to the man, but he also understood that he would never walk the decks of a warship in service again if that happened.

And might just go ahead and retire at that point anyway, a jinx on all commanding officers.

"Status?" Waters asked.

"Wounded civilian, per Nevin," Narayana replied. "He invoked an Emergency Protocol, so serious enough to matter. Past that, I don't know, save that he had Perry and two of his people with him."

Roland slipped into the little radio room forward without another word. Narayana didn't mind. And extra set of hands right now might matter.

He'd been counting in his head. Boyce got her little truck

launched a little faster than he'd expected, at a moment when it might matter, so he simply nodded to himself.

Expert Sailor Porter Zavaleta appeared.

"Sir?" he asked.

"Ask Veillon to unlock the armory," Narayana replied to the man's unasked question. "You and Diseth set a watch on the tower just in case."

The sailing notes for Jaffa's Corner had mentioned it being a rough place. Not exactly civilized, but not beholden to anyone else, either.

Outside of *A'Zedi* space, which meant that he wasn't supposed to enforce any laws unless asked by planetary authorities.

Narayana could, however, defend the ship. Using ship's particle cannon in an atmosphere was bad, but he still had a railgun pulsar he could use, small supersonic metal spheres that converted kinetic energy to destruction when dealing with incoming missiles.

Or low-flying troublemakers.

Whatever Maddox had gotten himself into, Narayana would find out soon enough. And figure out how to protect the man.

A'Zedi Survey Corps was *First In The Field*. That often meant alone and a long ways from help, far more often than any other Commands ever faced.

It made one self-contained.

He was going to need that today.

THREE

Maddox had the woman in his arms as he got through the front door, across the short porch, and two steps down to a road that had never been more than graveled occasionally. Asphalt cost tax money. And required regular touch up by dedicated gear.

Sixteen millimeter gravel could be dumped from a moving vehicle, scraped more or less flat, and mashed down by traffic.

Easy, and didn't require much in the way of working local government.

Kinda like most of Jaffa's Corner appeared to operate.

He wasn't surprised when Broom and Bachchan both drew Adjustable Disruptors. Miniature, handheld particle cannons.

Maddox didn't ask if they were twisted to stun or kill. He'd let his three experts handle that decision. That was their profession. He was merely their commander.

Broom walked close, eyes forward and a hand on the woman's stomach holding a compress. Maddox could feel her blood dripping down his hip, warm and sluggish. Her eyes were open and tracking him, but not entirely focused.

"We'll get you to safety," he told her again as she seemed to recognize him.

Or at least recognize him as someone who hadn't just been trying to kill her.

She nodded, eyes filled with stoic sternness floating on top of a stomach wound that had to hurt.

In the distance, a flash of light from the direction of the port, up and over like a mortar round. *Packrat.* The sound arrived a moment later.

"That's my gun," a man yelled.

Maddox turned back to look.

"And you can have it back one bullet at a time," Perry snarled back evenly, bringing it up and aiming. "One. Two."

He didn't get to three, because the man threw himself back through the door into the bar, slamming the front door emphatically.

Others on the street suddenly decided to be elsewhere, turning and madly bolting for whatever shop or alley was closest when Bachchan and Broom pointed weapons up and down the long street.

Hopefully, he wasn't about to get a bad rep around here, but honestly, being too nice might be worse than stomping a few punks into the gravelly mud at his feet.

Place had that kind of feel.

And he hadn't seen a single gendarme of any kind since he landed.

Boyce knew her shit. *Packrat* dropped, loud and low on thrusters at the intersection, then came towards him at a fast walk before settling and cutting power. Maddox was already in motion, understanding that he would walk the slowest with this load.

The triangle around him kept pace. He got to the bed of

Packrat, planted a foot on a bumper, and thrust himself and his cargo up and over the sides before he put her carefully down. Broom stayed right with him. Bachchan and Perry were back to back, supervising the street in case someone around here thought that their opinions mattered.

"Go!" he yelled, but Boyce already had her engines rumbling, then cut power in and lifted off smoothly.

Didn't get high. Probably wouldn't scorch any roofs because she was moving at a high lateral speed back to the starport. Bachchan had bumped Maddox out of the way and was helping Broom tape the woman's wounds, front and back when they rolled her up on her side.

Lots of blood, but those two weren't frantic. Maddox took his cues from that and relaxed a little.

"What is that?" he asked Perry, pointed at the gun.

"Semi-automatic of some sort," the Squire replied. "Self-contained cartridges in the handle. Gunpowder ignites and sends a small ball of spinning metal downrange at supersonic speed. Think they are loaded with simple ball ammunition, because it went right though him without bouncing or ripping everything out on the way."

"Her," Maddox corrected him. "This is a woman."

Perry looked closer, then shrugged. A lot of folks joined the military because they didn't like bullies like *Wronlori*. Saw themselves as protectors. Didn't matter who.

Perry was another one. He handed Maddox back the weapon, after flipping the safety on with his thumb. Maddox let the weight settle himself.

Then they were to the ship. Boyce would have gotten yelled at by some commanders for the speed with which she approached and dropped into *Packrat*'s tiny flight bay, but he appreciated it today.

Doc Nordin was there with a medical bag as soon as the engines cut and the exhaust smoke got sucked out of the small bay by fans.

Perry grabbed Bachchan and vanished. Broom moved to help Nordin. A quick dermal injection he presumed for pain, then Nordin brought out her Quasiprobe.

Emergency Medical Intensive Care Technician, because a ship as small as *Doctor Kay* didn't rate a formal doctor. Or even a nurse. Still, good enough to run the machines that handled a lot of the formal diagnostics, plus maintain and distribute the usual medicines for hangovers and pulled muscles. Broken bones were rare, but could be splinted or cast as needed in the field, depending. Bullet wounds were unique, in his experience or even his knowledge.

She stopped and looked up at him.

"Bullets?" she asked.

Maddox didn't have a holster, so he held up the weapon for her to see, then tucked it into a pocket as she spoke.

"Okay, surgery machine," she said. "Serge, lift her up."

"I've got it," Maddox said, squatting. "Already covered in blood here."

And he got the stranger lifted.

Less pain in the woman's eyes as the painkiller took effect. Maddox stepped over and down while the other two watched.

"Broom, clear the corridors," Nordin ordered.

She could do that in a medical emergency, but Broom wouldn't have argued with the woman.

Down one deck to main level, then down another and through enlisted crew spaces, everyone standing politely with space down the middle as he carried the stranger forward and rested her in medbay. Nordin started deploying her robots and Maddox stepped back.

"You need me for anything, Doc?" he asked.

"Negative, sir," she said without looking up from a screen.

"Then I'm going to get clean," he announced. "Update me later when you know more."

And he left.

Maddox was pretty certain that Coxswain Laux could get all the blood out of this uniform and his boots. If not, he'd recycle this set and call it good.

Narayana Yadav would need an update, but it could wait for now.

FOUR

Narayana had watched on screens, rather than get in the way. Deck Officer was supposed to be in charge of the boat anyway, with the Knight Commanding merely making executive decisions and exercising oversight.

Everyone here answered to Narayana first.

Thus, he had remotely watched Boyce's pickup and return. Witnessed Maddox carry a wounded civilian to medical. Noted that the man went and showered before anything else.

Narayana had fresh coffee from the map room, but was staying on the bridge, mostly to stay in sight of everyone suddenly on duty and prepared for whatever emergency was coming next.

Survey Corps. If you wanted a boring life, you should have gone into Construction Command.

Maddox showed up just about exactly when Narayana had expected. Damp hair. Fresh uniform. Smelled the coffee and nodded, stepping into the map room and having the machine brew him a batch.

Narayana waited, focused on his breathing. And making sure his hands didn't shake.

Much.

Maddox returned with a mug in one hand. Looked at Narayana. Paused, lips pressed together.

"Hadn't realized how all that might hit you," he said. "Sorry about that."

And that, right there, was why the whole crew liked Maddox Nevin. He stopped, watched, and learned. Understood that his deck officer might have a little PTSD over the whole situation.

Narayana shrugged and grabbed the mug tighter.

"What happened?" he asked in a voice trying to be casual.

"Woman in the bar was suddenly mobbed by a handful of locals," Maddox replied. "We started to intervene and it turned into a full brawl. Somebody shot her with a gunpowder firearm, so we proceeded to beat the unholy crap out of all of them, then got the woman to safety. Not like the locals could be trusted."

"Outsider, yes," Narayana replied. "What are we doing with her?"

"Saving her life," the Knight replied evenly.

Not that Narayana was surprised. Maddox was like that. Most of them were, but the Knight embodied it in ways that the rest of the crew only aspired to, most days.

"How long do the computers say something like this takes to heal?" Maddox asked, still standing in the doorway to the map room.

Narayana typed a few commands and reviewed the results.

"Where was she hit?" he asked.

"Stomach area," Maddox replied. "Didn't hit bone. Went all the way through cleanly, near as I could tell."

"As fast as you got her to the medical robots, maybe as little as two weeks," Narayana said. "Maybe twice that, if organ damage is severe. Interestingly, time to care appears to be the most critical factor, and she was in surgery in eight minutes."

He caught Maddox's nod. Saved her life, indeed. Sounded like she might have been left to bleed out and die on the street if he hadn't gotten involved.

"What?" Maddox asked, catching Narayana's sour thought obviously.

"How long were we supposed to be on Jaffa's World?" Narayana asked.

"Crap," Maddox muttered. "Less than that. Same time, she won't be up to protecting herself from those men for a month. If then. I think they might get ugly next time."

"Shooting her wasn't ugly?"

"Okay, point," Maddox acceded. "We might have a stray on our hands for a bit. You stay on top of things here. I need to look up all the relevant rules and regulations for a situation like this."

"Probably comes down to you making a decision and hoping command backs you up," Narayana pointed out.

"Hopefully, they will," he said, stepping back into the map room.

Narayana contained his sigh and went back to his watch for now.

What was coming next?

FIVE

Maddox was reading the Code on a tablet when a shadow appeared at the door to the map room.

"Sir?" Squire Perry asked.

Maddox put his reader down and rubbed his eyes. Not a lot to go on. Mostly commander's decision. And responsibility.

"What do you have, Squire?" he asked the tall man.

Perry took a step into the room and put the tip of the woman's walking stick on the table. A little under a meter and a half in length. Wood, polished and smooth. Stained almost as dark as cherry.

Looking closer, it was flat on the sides. Perry grabbed about a third of the way down and pulled the end, separating it into two pieces, one of which was a metal blade, sharpened on one side and the back thirty or so centimeters from the tip. Wasn't steel. Color was wrong. Too dark gray, in spite of being polished. Contained and hidden inside a scabbard made to look like a walking stick.

"Oh?" Maddox asked as Perry held the two pieces up.

"She could have drawn and done some serious damage with this thing," the man replied.

"What's the metal?"

"Haven't asked Engineering to get involved yet, sir," Perry said. "Wasn't sure it was my place. Mostly wanted you aware. Presuming I should store it in the armory when we come back down from alert?"

"Down?" Maddox perked up.

What had he missed?

"The Armiger decided to maintain the armed watch topside," Perry nodded. "Just in case someone decided to get rambunctious."

Maddox could see that. Not that an armed mob was likely, but folks might get a little pissy after they'd beaten up a bar and threatened the bartender. He had, anyway. Probably shouldn't go into town for a few days, letting folks recover. Maybe send someone to scout the place, except that his two best urban scouts, Broom and Bachchan, had already blown their covers.

"Go ahead and put that in the armory, yes," Maddox decided. "I'll check with your boss about the alert schedule."

"Very good, sir." And Perry was gone.

He still had the pistol in his cabin, stored in his personal safe for now. It probably needed to go to the armory as well, but it could wait.

Maddox considered the sword instead. Sharp. Lethal. And he'd seen her take one person down without killing them in the process. Maybe she hadn't needed his help?

Water under the bridge. She needed it now. And the regulations were pretty vague.

He rose and stepped out to the bridge again. Narayana nodded as he went by and Maddox stuck his head into the

Radio room. Waters was on duty, instead of one of his enlisted people.

"Sir?"

"Keep an ear out on any local communications frequencies," Maddox ordered, sorry that he didn't have Nyssa Taggart with him, and her ability to hack civilian codes pretty easily.

Of course, they'd given her some amazingly powerful tools to do that with.

"What am I looking for, sir?" Waters asked.

Maddox paused to consider the order before it became official, written down for everyone standing this watch.

"Assume that the locals might be upset at us for any of a number of reasons, some of which won't make any sense," he said, going ahead and damning the torpedoes on this one. "Look for anyone mentioning us by any identifiable characteristic, such as name, nationality, or size. Pay attention to suggestions of violence or trouble, next time we're in town. Route it to your boss, Deck Officer, or me, depending on who is awake. Sound an alarm if you think it warrants immediate action. Clear enough?"

"Aye, sir," Waters said, shoulders coming forward and down as he started typing furiously.

Maddox stepped back and walked over to his Second-In-Command.

"A lot of potential false positives, I know," Maddox said quietly. "Waters and his people are sharp enough to filter it. And we can always overreact now. I'd prefer that to underreacting until it was too late."

"Understood," Narayana replied. "Just got a note from Nordin that her patient is out of surgery and into recovery."

"Good," Maddox said. "I'll go see what that implies and update you."

Technically, Maddox was supposed to issue orders to his crew and have them handle things, but he'd gotten them into this mess in the first place, so it wasn't fair to ask them to cover his ass without him helping.

If he had a stray, for how long?

SIX

Liselott Nordin had described herself more than once as a former horsegirl who had enlisted to escape the farm, and because she hadn't been able to afford Veterinary Medicine school, so she'd gone into human medicine instead. The *A'Zedi* navy didn't have many critters. Nor did the land forces that she had ever encountered, fleet or civilian auxiliary.

Today, she'd kinda stepped everything up a notch. Nothing beyond her capabilities, but well past her experience, even with the robots doing most of the work and her having the manual open as she walked through the whole process.

Inspect the wound. Through and through, punching the small intestine but not bouncing off a hip or rib in the process. Clean and debride the wound on both sides. Disinfect everything after getting her stripped bare.

Spare woman. Skinny, but wiry muscles. Like Lise's old friend Jules who had done barrel racing and roping for a while before getting married. And only developing curves later.

This one had no curves. Lots of scars. Clean and straight,

suggesting blades instead of bullets. Lise figured she could ask later.

Right now, she'd gone in and sewn and glued things shut where they should be. Treated the whole abdominal cavity with more stuff to keep her healthy. Given her a couple of different chemicals to help accelerate healing.

All the stuff the book said to do. About all that was missing was Grandma's chicken soup, but Lise hadn't figure out how to bribe or blackmail Cordell into making a batch. That, or maybe she needed to go to his boss and ask Squire Grippen, who was technically Chef of the boat, while Cordell was only a Cook.

Purser Buccheri was an asshole, so she wouldn't bother asking him. Better to sneak around the officers, probably.

Which was why she started and squeaked when she looked up and the commander was standing in the door, eyeing her silently.

Shit, talk about hand in the cookie jar.

"Sir?" she managed, only slightly hyperventilating.

"Came to check on your customer, Doc," he replied. "She okay? Are you okay?"

"Sir, yes, sir," Lise replied automatically. "Was just thinking about feeding her in a few days when she wakes up and is ready. Nothing for a day except in intravenous drip to keep her hydrated, but the woman has no body fat at all, so she'll need something a little sooner than most."

His eyes didn't seem to miss anything. Lise flashed back to that one dream where she was walking the halls of her old high school naked, about to take a test.

And the blush was so hard she felt like she was about to pass out.

"Sit," he ordered, pointing.

She did. Focused on the in and out. Got her heart kinda aimed in the right direction.

Helped that Knight Nevin ignored her and walked over to read the medboard over the patient's bed.

"Gear?" he asked.

Took her a moment to process.

"Oh, under the bed in a footlocker, sir," Lise replied. "Had a belt with several pouches. Shirt was a loss, both of them. Pants went to the Cox' for cleaning. Shoes, too."

He nodded and knelt, pulling the box out and opening it.

Thing was kinda like a gunbelt. Around the hips instead of the waist. Big pouch on the right side that strapped down. Smaller ones all the way around. Lise hadn't done an inventory, too busy with surgery and recovery.

Commander stood up and opened the big pouch, rifling around before closing it again. First pouch left of the buckle had whatever he was looking for. Lise had risen unconsciously and stepped close, having to look around his arm because the Knight was tall while she was short. She had lotsa muscles. No height to go with them.

"Sir?"

"Think this is her papers, Doc," he said. "Mark that I checked it out and will have it either in my safe or return it to you, once I open it and see what's inside."

Lise held her tongue. Technically correct, but she found the mystery kinda biting her hiney.

Who was this woman? And how had she managed to get shot in a bar? And done so in a way that the commander was immediately there and got her here and into surgery fast enough to really matter?

She'd ask Yadav later. He liked her enough to maybe gossip.

If he knew anything. Look in Nevin's face wasn't promising.

SEVEN

Maddox was in his office. Certain things that he didn't need to share with the crew at the moment. He'd cleared his desk, then spread things out as he removed them from the wallet and flattened them out.

Money in a variety of currencies. ID papers identifying her as Toshiko Hajós. Birth registered on Metra and a citizen of the *Holy Imperium of Copez*, except that her coloration was wrong.

Copez tended to be darker than *Traisa* or *Wronlori* in skin tone, while lighter than *A'Zedi* citizens like him. At least on average.

Hajós was lighter than almost anyone he'd encountered. Almost porcelain skin. At the same time, jet black hair darker than his, so not an albino, either. Straight hair, too, instead of having a little wave like his. Long enough to pull into a tail at her neck, but unbraided today.

No gray in her hair, so he was willing to believe her papers identifying her as twenty-nine. Basically his age. But not an ethnotype he knew, not that he'd spent much time focusing on the *Holy Imperium*.

Instead, he had commissioned into Fleet Operations, before a transfer to Transport Command that he'd tried so hard to get out of, but had been the best thing to ever happen to him, landing him on *Marrakesh* under Captain Boru. Now Survey Corps, but on a different frontier.

Maddox sighed and dialed a number on his intercom. Armiger Freya Vilchis, ship's Diplomat.

"Sir?" she appeared quickly, maybe a touch nervous, but everybody had been knocked a little off center today and might require a few to recover.

"The *Holy Imperium of Copez*, Madam Diplomat," he said simply.

Woman was smart. Highly charismatic, too, able to turn *bubbly* on and off like a switch, but he needed her brains.

"Aye?" she pressed.

"I figure I need a quick briefing on *Copez*," Maddox said. "And then later either a deeper dive or a recommendation for a book I should be reading. Our guest is from *Copez*, but not the standard ethnotype I'm familiar with, so I'd like to dig deeper and don't really know their culture or civilization beyond a fairly superficial layer. Can you be prepared to give a brief talk to the officers over dinner? Figure we'll all need an update, and this saves you from doing it more than once."

"Where in *Copez*?" she asked. "That might matter."

Maddox paused to find the document again.

"Planet named Metra," he replied.

"Excellent, sir," she replied, looking down at a clock no doubt. "Three hours? I'll have something."

"Good," Maddox replied. "Thank you."

He cut the line and circled back. Money. Papers. A few pictures of the woman and few friends or possibly family. She held that staff sword in about half of the images, so it was important to her, but he wasn't certain what it implied. A few other mementos that made no sense to Maddox at all, so he carefully put it all back in the wallet, closed it up with a leather cord that wrapped around a button, and rose to put it into the ship's safe behind his desk.

It was a mystery. And he might have saved the woman's life. At the same time, he might have been the reason she got shot, when a mob of sailors suddenly decided to jump in.

Woman carrying a sword everywhere she went might not have needed the help.

He'd ask her when she woke up.

And apologize.

EIGHT

Sitting down to dinner with the officers, Freya Vilchis figured that she probably had the broadest education of anyone on the boat. Practical side effect of being the ship's official Diplomat. The others all went deep into a single hole in the ground. Engineering. Combat. Command. Something.

She had to be prepared to talk to random strangers on any planet they might be sent. In whatever gear or garb might be culturally appropriate, which had once included absolutely nothing except leather sandals and a hair tie.

Freya knew she was pretty. Dark brown skin utterly without blemish. Black hair with just enough wave to offset the heavy thickness. She possibly could have been a model if she'd been taller, but she was merely average height. That had also worked to her advantage more than once, when she'd been able to bat her eyes at someone to defuse a situation.

But the Knight had asked for specific information. Freya had gotten all the scuttlebutt from Narayana and Perry, but all they knew was what had happened.

Not what Nevin intended.

Still, she had a pretty deep encyclopedia here, dedicated to cultures and languages, so she'd been able to locate Metra.

Freya looked around the wardroom, she noted that almost everyone was here tonight. Commander and Deck Officer. Her representing the Diplomacy Section, with Rolland standing anchor watch right now by his request.

Kjell Forslund and Camden Morgan from Engineering. Joy Kimmel and Astrid Calder from Hull Division. Petra Veillon and Steve Perry from Weapons. Purser Buccheri that nobody really liked, but not enough to socially ostracize.

Even Squire Sigun Grippen was technically cooking, but had left the window to the kitchen open to listen if she spoke up.

Folks were eating a pasta in white sauce with shrimp added. Traveled well over astronomical distances and packed a lot of protein and calories into a small package. Nevin had even broken out some wine tonight, which made it a special event.

"I've asked Veillon to brief us on *Copez*," Nevin began around bites. "First, I figured I would bring everybody up to date on what happened with me and Perry this morning in town. All shore leave will be canceled for a few days, and that's my fault, so we might also leave early and find someplace friendlier."

Freya sat back and listened as he continued. Maddox Nevin wasn't a natural storyteller, but at the same time he had a gift for clarity in his speech that conveyed things cleanly. She was in the bar when the brawl started. She was there, taking that pistol away from someone. She and her friends taking out an angry mob and kicking its ass, before rescuing the princess.

"From there, we got her back here and into surgery," he concluded. "Nordin has her under sedation and observation, but is confident in a full recovery. Because she's from *Copez*, but not an ethnotype I'm familiar with, I asked Veillon for help."

"What is she?" Forslund asked.

"Pale," Nevin replied. "Practically white. Black, straight hair."

Freya nodded. That made more sense now. Nevin turned to her.

"You ready to brief your crazy commanding officer?" he asked with a smile.

She shared it. As did several others. He reminded them all of Kumar Das that way.

"Metra was the key, sir," she began. "That world is part of the *Holy Imperium*, but only physically."

"Oh?"

"A century ago, it was the capital world of the *Amaechi Concordancy*, before they got absorbed by *Copez*."

"Absorbed," he replied darkly.

Freya nodded.

"A fairly brutal war of conquest was required," she explained. "But *Copez* had superior technology and that was enough to overwhelm *Amaechi* and subjugate them."

"Modern problems?" he pressed, like they were alone in the room, with everyone else holding their breaths.

"Exactly the opposite of what one might expect," Freya countered.

"How so?"

"The former royal family was legally exiled," Freya told them. "Hostages on Igen, the *Copez* capital world. Supposedly well treated, but never allowed to go home again."

"With you so far," Nevin nodded, eyes dark and focused.

"After the conquest was completed, a significant portion of the former elite nobility chose a form of exile as well," she continued. "They retain ties to Metra in the form of land and property. And they register births there as a matter of course and Imperium record, but tend to live semi-permanently aboard starships that trade along that entire frontier. As a rule, however, they do not ever cross the frontier to space outside what is claimed by *Copez*. Some of the folks I looked up today hint that leaving *Copez* might cause them to be denied reentry later, depending."

"Where is Metra?" Narayana asked curiously.

"Farthest side of *Copez*," she replied automatically. "About as far from Horwin and the rest of *A'Zedi* as you can get and still be in civilized space. There are worlds beyond the current borders of the *Holy Imperium*, but they tend to be newer colonies or renegades who would prefer to remain *Unaffiliated*."

Nevin whistled.

"She is a long ways from home, then," he offered.

"Do we know why?" Freya asked.

Everything up until now had been purely academic research. Digging into various things and following rabbit holes as new ideas cropped up.

"Nothing," Nevin replied. "Situation started with the confrontation."

"*We don't like your kind around here*," Perry suddenly spoke up, mimicking someone. "That was what he said. *You need to go back where you belong*. They knew she was a stranger. I mean, easy enough to look at her and see that, seeing as how dark the rest of us are in this region of space, but that kinda went beyond simple racism, if you ask me."

Freya nodded. So did the rest. *A'Zedi* tended to be fairly dark. Not the deepest 100% chocolate in tone, but seventy to ninety percent was the normal range. *Copez* was lighter. *Wronlori* blond and golden.

Then there was this pale stranger.

Freya started to say something when the intercom beeped loud enough to override conversation.

"Alert," someone spoke. "Deck Officer to the conning tower. Repeat, Deck Officer to the conning tower. All hands stand by to repel boarders."

Freya heard the words, but they made no sense to her. The others, however, we all up and running for the hatch, so she fell into their wake.

Boarders?

NINE

Maddox had been closest to the door, and managed to get out ahead of everyone except Perry, which didn't surprise him. Man moved fast when he had to.

Maddox paused in his quarters long enough to grab that slugthrower and carry it in a pocket as he got to the bridge and went up the spiral staircase to the top deck.

You could fly the ship from up here, but only in emergency situations. Instead, it was usually a patio for events on a nice night, with a small operations station tucked in that could be accessed if you needed to sail the ship across water on thrusters, since it could land on water or land.

They were on solid earth today. Nightfall.

Were those *torches* burning? Seriously?

Perry was there. Yadav had the bridge when Maddox went by. Several more armed sailors had appeared, spreading out over the top of the ship. The vessel was a long, rounded rectangle, viewed from either end. No cover but the conning tower itself, and Maddox spotted Specialist Trinity Diseth fully atop it with a longarm of some sort, tucked in and aimed at the crowd.

Broom and Bachchan were flat on the deck here, also pointing weapons outward. Porter Zavaleta and Vanya Dowe were watching the ends and back against any flanking infiltration.

Maddox stepped close enough to Perry to talk without yelling, but not so close that someone shooting from down there would have an easy time. Plus, it was largely dark up here because someone had killed the lights on the top of the ship while leaving the landing lights on below.

Added something of an ominous tone, coming up from the ground.

"What's going on?" Maddox asked generally, unsure who might answer.

"Radio caught a signal of a mob marching, sir," Broom replied from his spot. "Wasn't sure what it was, so let us know. Figured that they were just being punks in town, but they walked from downtown to the starport gates and kept going. Since we're the only ones over here, it was pretty easy to see they were coming for us. I hit the alert signal and figured I could get yelled at later for being a sissy. But they kept coming."

"You did exactly right, Serge," Maddox replied, studying the mass of people below.

Maybe a hundred people or so. Hard to see faces except by torchlight, but someone had honest-to-gods taken some sticks and wrapped cloth or something, then lit it on fire. Barbaric, but effective, since it added a level of menace that mere flashlights wouldn't have carried.

"That is close enough!" Perry yelled in a voice of **DOOM!** that echoed off a couple of distant hulls.

And he had a Disruptor Bombardier in his hands, the carbine version of the Adjustable Disruptor that the others were aiming. Pointed at the crowd.

Vanya Dowe was qualified on the Light Disruptor Cannon,

like Trinh Lành Hoàng had done, back on *Marrakesh*. Maddox wondered if he should go ahead and let Perry bring it out in certain situations in the future. A bipod-mounted anti-vehicle weapon might get folks' attention.

Then the railgun pulsar mount on the top of the conning tower deployed, up and rotating over until it was pointed at the heart of the mob with a squeal of metal on metal that normally indicated some failure of maintenance, but tonight sounded like a harpy summoning you to your day of reckoning.

Two centimeter steel spheres, accelerated by a magnetic coil to excessive speeds. Maddox had never considered them on the ground as a defense element, but apparently someone below him had.

And the mob suddenly shivered and took a step back, so the warning served its purpose.

Maddox could only imagine what opening fire with such a thing might be like here, if it came to that.

Hopefully, it wouldn't, because the mob entity below him had broken, and turned back into a crowd. Still angry, but no longer a singular creature.

He could work with this, but only from up here.

"I will use lethal force to defend my vessel," Maddox yelled down, mostly to establish to whoever thought otherwise what they should be expecting if they kept coming.

Jaffa's World was *Unaffiliated*. And not all that well organized in and of itself. Bunch of fiercely independent folks who didn't want much government telling them what to do.

He'd rely on firepower.

"We want the girl!" some man yelled back.

Others growled agreement.

"No," Maddox said, letting his volume fall and forcing them to quiet down some if they wanted a conversation.

He was backlit by darkness in a dark uniform, so difficult to pick out. They were lit up like day by landing floods.

And Maddox had no doubts that someone raising a weapon to shoot at him would get shitstormed by his people.

"She's not your kind!" someone else yelled from a different part of the mob.

"You going to rape her before you kill her or after?" Maddox snarled back at them. "I don't see any other reason you folks got all hot and bothered to come over here making demands."

"Her kind aren't welcome!"

"You will walk away," Maddox ordered simply. "Or we will open fire and slaughter all of you. I am in fear for my life from an armed mob. *A'Zedi* will probably pin a medal on my chest. Hell, your own government might reward me for cleaning up the streets around here killing all of you."

That elicited an ugly growl, but no forward motion. Then somebody shifted the aiming point of the railgun, because it squealed again and the nearest edge of the crowd flinched back. Tried to step back, but couldn't because folks behind them were pushing forward. They turned around and started yelling and fussing at one another to move.

That escalated sideways, because punches started being thrown as the crowd fell in on itself.

Maddox didn't duck back, but did step sideways until the conning tower partially obscure his silhouette. Perry stayed out in the open, but he was aiming at someone, as was everyone else Maddox could see.

The fight below turned into another bar brawl. Almost a pie fight, had there been any handy, but it didn't quite verge over into the comical.

Until Yadav or someone suddenly sounded the launch

sirens. Skull-splitting sound, but it had the desired effect, because suddenly everyone on the ground was running for their lives to get away before thruster exhaust started cooking them.

In fact, that didn't even sound like the dumbest thing Maddox had heard all day.

He turned to Perry.

"Clear the decks for launch," Maddox said simply, then went into the tower and down the stairs.

TEN

Stenny Kellogg was still getting used to the thought that she could be an officer. Apparently, the commander had known a woman on his old boat who had been identified as soon as she first enlisted, and sent to officer's school, then commissioned at nineteen.

And Knight Nevin spoke of Nyssa Taggart in almost reverential terms, so he must have liked her.

With the alert, she'd taken the piloting station and brought everything live. Standard procedure. Everything ready but locked down for the Deck Officer's orders.

"Kellogg, sound the launch sirens," Armiger Yadav announced.

She couldn't help the flinch. Or the turn over her shoulder, wide-eyed.

"We're not launching," he smiled at her. "I want them running."

Oh.

And he'd already ordered the railgun teams to aim at the

crowd. Man wasn't messing around today, because their weapon was live right now.

She pushed the button. Heard the sirens wind up and then back down. Anyone on the ship would know launch was imminent. As would everyone within about a kilometer or more, depending on weather.

Cool clear night outside, so maybe three kilometers.

"Good, there they go," the Deck Officer announced.

Stenny was focused on her controls, but clicked a button and added a small external view to one of her screens.

People, going away assholes and elbows. Good.

Who the hell storms a navy ship in dry harbor? And one that's armed?

Steps coming down from above turned out to be the Knight.

"Excellent work, all of you," he announced as he moved to stand over her shoulder. "Yadav, anybody ashore right now?"

"Negative, sir," Deck Officer replied. "Strict orders to remain aboard until further notice. Seemed smarter than waiting."

"Agreed one hundred percent," Nevin said. "Kellogg, initiate launch sequence. I'm fine if it takes longer than usual. And tell Forslund that you're acting on my orders directly when he bitches."

And she figured he would. Engineer was a little fussy about his machines. Still, the launch alert siren should have given him a clue.

She opened a line aft.

"Engineering this is the bridge," she said, striving for calm and collected. "Bring all systems live for launch. Repeat, bring all systems live for launch."

Stenny cut the line before any of the profanities made it

back to her, but she was pretty sure they were there. Might hear them later. They could talk to the two officers supervising her right now if there was a serious problem.

Yellow lights slowly started turning green as generators came on and locked into sequence. Thruster systems began heating up and charging fuel lines. Reactors got awakened from their slumbers like grouchy trolls. And mechanics.

Took about five minutes instead of two, but this was a cold start launch, and the commander hadn't sounded the ship-wide alert for crash operations, so they were probably taking their time aft.

Nevin or Yadav could always open a comm and yell at them to hurry, but the starport was utterly abandoned now, everyone hauling ass to get clear of her launch zone before they got barbecued.

Doctor Kay was by herself.

"Ground Control, this is *A'Zedi* Survey Corvette *Kalyn Blackford*," she said into the radio. "Ground launch imminent. Flight path filed."

Again, she cut the line before the profanities. Ground people over yonder were probably more in shock than her engineers. Events weren't about to make those all warm and fuzzy either tonight.

"Deck Officer, I have green boards," she announced finally, about the time she was set to fire a few profanities of her own aft to get them off their asses.

"Confirm green boards, Pilot," Yadav replied. "Stand by to launch."

Stenny toggled the last few controls into the up position, hands poised.

"Pilot, take us to orbit and hold there," Knight Nevin ordered, so apparently they were serious about this.

Automatic for her. Top closed up with everyone confirmed inside. Hatches locked. Thrusters warm. Fuel systems behaving. Scanners showing clear sky to the stars overhead.

Stenny lifted off.

Part of her wondered about the civilian they had rescued this morning, but obviously this wasn't a safe place for her. And the commander had decided that maybe it wasn't safe for any *A'Zedi* crew members, either.

Pity, as she'd been looking forward to walking about on the surface at some point.

But this was the navy.

Maybe next time.

ELEVEN

Narayana had joined Maddox in the map room. *Doctor Kay* was clear at the outer bounds of orbital space above Jaffa's World. Drifting, but not leaving just yet.

Poised, as it were.

"Now, what?" Narayana asked.

"I don't figure that either of us were bluffing down there," Maddox replied with a hard smile.

"I did clear the defensive teams to fire, but only on my order," Narayana shrugged.

"File a maintenance report that the system needs oiling, because is squeaks pretty loudly," Maddox said, still grinning. "That was useful, but I don't want it freezing on us next time we need it."

"Noted," Narayana replied. "Probably the only time in the service history of this boat when that's to our benefit. Where are we going?"

Maddox grimaced.

"Rules and regulations don't cover a situation like this," he replied. "*Commander's Judgment* seems to be about all I can rely on. Given what just happened on the ground, I'm inclined to believe that none of us were safe staying behind, so this won't cause you much trouble. I might get yelled at, but I might not. And she'll be in bed for probably two weeks as she heals, even with everything Nordin can do."

"You thinking about completing the survey run?" Narayana asked.

Not entirely surprised. They'd lifted off from Vhogga originally with several extra crates of communications relays and sensor buoys to go with everything loaded into their Vertical Launch System bays. The first half had already been deployed, which had gotten them clear out into the nothingness of Jaffa's World, where Maddox had decided to spend a few days showing the flag before circling back.

Not nearly as friendly a place as Astarte III. He'd put that down to social isolation. At least Astarte III had a lot of trade flowing through it, kind of linking *A'Zedi* and *Wronlori* worlds without direct connection.

Everyone there got to pretend that there wasn't a war going on.

He studied Maddox's face.

"I think that two weeks lets us finish the run, yes," Knight Nevin replied. "She'll be awake and coherent long before that, but not in shape to go anywhere, I don't think. Maybe we drop her somewhere. Maybe we take her with us to Astarte III. Dunno. Don't have to know right now. Original mission is half-done, and we're in a position to finish it."

Narayana shrugged. Survey Corps work wasn't always exciting, though he suspected that living around Maddox Nevin might be. Like Kumar had been.

At the same time, the equipment they were deploying would help connect more worlds. Or spot *Wronlori* fleets intent on causing trouble. Something. About half of them got destroyed on a regular basis, presumably by smugglers and pirates who didn't want records kept.

Thus, *Doctor Kay* out servicing and delivering more.

He watched Maddox click on the intercom.

"Astronomer here," Dr. Sabeen Abbas was there instantly.

"It's Knight Nevin," Maddox told him. "We're going to go ahead and complete the second half of the deployments from here. This is your notice to get everything checked out."

"Understood, sir," Abbas replied. "Kind of assumed something along those lines. We'll be ready."

Maddox cut the line and studied him for a moment. Narayana worked at not flinching, but this day had still gone so utterly sideways that he was off-kilter. And hadn't had a chance to talk to Nordin yet about something to sleep tonight.

"I don't know that our guest needs to be secured," Maddox said quietly. "At the same time, we don't know anything useful about her, or how she might react to the situation."

"She might have left clothing and things on the planet," Narayana nodded. "Except that I wouldn't trust anything not in my immediate control, from what you and the others have said about that town. Bandit kind of place. Especially as racist as they turned out to be."

"Exactly," Maddox told him. "You and Perry sort out whatever needs to be done. I'd like her under constant observation, but not locked in a cabin unless it becomes necessary. You figure out where that line is, and blame me for everything when she complains."

"You think she will?"

"Wake up on a strange ship, functionally kidnapped, having been shot in a bar fight?" Maddox asked. "Sure, we can explain it to her, but we've certain stripped her of most of her agency at the moment, however necessary it was in the moment. I'd like to fix that later. Keeping her calm enough to explain will help. Keeping the crew from bothering her, and vice versa, until she and I can talk is my next mission."

"I'll work with security and sort them out," Narayana replied.

"Excellent," Maddox said. "Thank you for cleaning up my mess."

Narayana started to say something, then shut up and nodded. Not a lot to say, because Maddox was taking responsibility. Not even Kumar had done that all the time, to say nothing of Avguri Senoky or Inari Kosere who had replaced him.

Narayana moved back to the bridge to issue orders to Kellogg and everyone else.

Then sort out what orders he and Perry needed to give.

PART 2
REFUGEE

TWELVE

Maddox had checked with Doc Nordin, so he knew the woman was awake, after two days in a medical coma to heal. Not chomping at the bit to get up and move yet, but that was probably coming soon.

Toshiko Hajós didn't look like a woman who stayed in bed one minute longer than necessary.

Her eyes locked on him like turrets as Maddox entered sick bay. Hard eyes. Blanket was up and he could see the top of a baggy shirt to keep her warm and covered, but the medic here was female, so that should help.

Still, Hajós had woken up in a strange room, surrounded by strangers, mostly nude and wounded.

Shitty situation. Still beat dead.

"I am Knight Maddox Nevin," he said quietly from the door, not moving inward just yet. "We rescued you after you were shot in the bar."

"I remember you carrying me," she replied quietly, a melodious voice with hints and burrs of a *Copez* accent underlain with something else.

Metra? *Amaechi Concordancy?* He didn't know.

"After surgery, while you were unconscious, a mob tried to attack my ship," he continued, taking a single step inward. "We drove them off, then decided that leaving Jaffa's World was probably safer for everyone, since the doc tells me that you might be in bed for a couple of weeks."

"Less than that," Hajós replied flatly.

"You need to heal first," Maddox countered. "Do none of us any good if you push too hard too soon and relapse. Plus, the ship is in deep space right now, on the way to complete our mission while we figured out what you needed."

"What I needed?" she asked.

Good, he'd confused her.

"Are there folks on Jaffa's World we need to contact and update about you and your location?" he asked.

"No, I have been traveling alone," Hajós replied.

"Whatever you had with you or on your belt is safe," Maddox continued. "I have your papers in my safe, and your sword is in the armory for now. The next question is where do we take you when we completed our mission?"

She blinked at him. Part of her confusion was certainly the pain killers Nordin had given her, but part of it had to be how weird the situation had gotten.

He could only imagine waking up like this, the roles reversed, and trying to make sense of it.

"Where will you take me?" she repeated his words carefully, eyes never leaving his.

"We're based out of Astarte III, an *Unaffiliated* world not far from *A'Zedi* space, much closer to the rim and a little anti-spinward from Jaffa's World," he nodded. "Normally, I'd be returning there after we completed our mission, but that's not necessarily the case here. I got the impression you weren't from

Jaffa's World, and given the way they reacted to you, I doubt you'd have been staying long."

Long pause. Measuring him, no doubt. Stranger. Strange ship. Wounded and alone.

"You are correct," she finally said. "But I am not certain what my next destination would have been from there."

Maddox replayed that in his head. And considered some of the other clues. FAR from home. Traveling alone. Armed.

Seeking someone?

"So I'm back to figuring out where you needed to go, since I kind of derailed all your plans," he told her. "And the medic still expects that you will need two weeks to heal, though you'll be able to walk some and start a sensible rehab before then. We're a Survey vessel, and my current mission involves deploying new buoys and repairing others, so those two weeks are accounted for from my end. If there is somewhere other than Astarte III where you want to be dropped off, you let me know."

"Why are you doing this, Knight Nevin?" she asked bluntly. Harshly, maybe, but he'd put that down to the stuff in her system for pain and healing.

He'd never been shot, but he'd had to be sedated a few times for routine stuff. Always came out tasting cotton for a day.

"It needed doing," Maddox told her. "Five on one weren't odds I liked."

"I could have handled them," she replied.

"Maybe," he split the emotional difference. "Then someone shot you in the stomach and I got the impression they would have left you to bleed out on the floor. That was the point I was required to act."

"Required?"

"Yes, ma'am," he nodded, automatically falling into parade rest, hands crossed behind his back.

She studied him. He waited.

Strangers, ill met. Her with absolutely no agency. Him with all of it and hers as well.

"What happens when we get somewhere?" she finally asked.

"You can walk down the gangplank and vanish, if that's your desire," Maddox told her. "Getting you there safe—wherever that is—is my geas."

He wasn't sure why his subconscious threw out that word, but it fit. And hit her like someone swatting her with a pillow from the flinch that ran all the way through her.

Maddox watched her mouth the word again, silently. He nodded.

And that sounded like as good an exit line as anyone had ever handed him, so he smiled, turned, and left before she could stop him.

Geas?

THIRTEEN

Maddox was in the map room that had turned into his primary office, more than the one forward where he officially did paperwork. It let the bridge crew access him with a loud question, while keeping him from breathing down necks and making them nervous. Kellogg was doing a lot better, but Specialist Sagan Dituri was still a little twitchy to have his commanding officer possibly keeping score.

Squire Perry appeared at the hatch. Maddox had gotten pretty good about not calling the man *Pretty*, a nickname he'd dubiously earned when an overzealous autocorrect function somewhere had updated his records that way and it had taken a bit before someone had caught it. Some of his crew were allowed to use the name, but Maddox was his commanding officer, and they were still sorting out that relationship. Might still get there at some point, but might not.

Man looked serious today. Stepped to the map room threshold, waited for a nod, then stepped in and closed the hatch behind him.

Maddox closed his tablet and waited.

"Coffee?" he asked, mostly to judge the level of concern he should be exhibiting.

"Probably," Perry replied, moving to the machine and fixing some.

So, somewhere in the middle. Important enough to walk up to main deck and close the hatch instead of simply sending an electronic message. Not an alert.

Maddox comported himself appropriately and watched the tall man work.

"Worried a little about Hajós, sir," he began as he moved to the table and set his mug down.

"Sit," Maddox ordered, waiting for him to comply. "What's she done?"

"Nothing," Perry replied. "Well, the usual bitching sailors do when confined to medbay and bored, but even less than my people. Instead, she's doing kata, both while in bed and when she can stand."

"Kata?" Maddox asked, confused.

"Martial arts training forms," Perry nodded. "Highly stylized. Usually done slowly as training and meditation. Sometimes under tension, sometimes not, usually depending on the base art studied."

"Gotcha," Maddox replied.

He'd seen Perry and others do such things, but he wasn't a close combat expert like this man. Nor did he have any particular interest.

Although...

How much better would it have been in a bar brawl, if he had? And he knew that Narayana had needed a couple of days to recover emotionally, having lost Kumar Das that way.

Maddox supposed that Perry and the others might wish he was more formally trained in that sort of thing if he was going to keep getting into trouble. He made a note to do some research before asking any questions.

"Okay?" he pressed.

"I've watched video that got recorded on security cams," Perry continued. "She's good."

"How good?"

"Exceptional," the man emphasized. "Might have been able to take those five in the bar."

"She a threat?" Maddox asked.

"Not today," Perry shook his head. "And not on this boat, where all the serious weapons are locked up and we could always lock her in a cabin if we had to. Most concerned that she might be a spy of some sort."

"Whose?" Maddox asked, only to get a shrug back.

"Diplomat says that she's unlikely to be a happy, little *Copez* citizen." Perry replied. "But a woman like that, traveling alone, dangerous, though I suppose the situation I've just described would require her to be dangerous. Do we know anything about her?"

"Only what I've managed so far," Maddox said. "And she's only been with us a week."

"Time to dig deeper, sir?" Perry pressed.

Maddox understood. Armiger Petra Veillon, the Gunner, was Perry's boss and head of the department, but she focused on ship's weapons. Perry and his people were specifically focused on ground operations. Bodyguards. Close combat.

Survey Corps was the tip of the spear. First in the Field. That mattered with them a lot more than Fleet Operations or Transport Command.

"Probably," Maddox replied. "I'll talk to the Chef and see if we can arrange something quiet. You have somebody serving as a steward, in case she does prove dangerous?"

"Thank you, sir," Perry said, picking up his mug and opening the hatch. "Load off my mind."

Maddox watched the empty space and considered. He had gotten daily reports from Nordin, indicating that Hajós was doing better. Healing just fine, with no setbacks.

And she'd had enough time to think, if she was up doing physical rehab training, in spite of Nordin wishing she'd spend more time horizontal and healing.

Everybody did it differently.

Still, she represented a mystery. One he'd stuck his nose into instead of leaving well enough alone.

And hindsight was an exact science.

Maddox rose. He'd head aft and chat with Grippen about a special meal for their special guest.

Or whatever it would turn out to be.

FOURTEEN

Maddox rose when Hajós was escorted into the officer's wardroom. She only moved a little stiffly, but didn't require Nordin to do anything except follow close and hover.

Her clothing had been replaced, but not until Jareth Laux, Ship's Costumer, had created her a new wardrobe in a similar pattern. Black pants. Gray crossover jacket that hung to her thighs, over a pale green T-shirt. Hair pulled back into a simple tie.

Without the pain, she wasn't beautiful, but attractive. Regular features. Dark eyes. Pale, inverted triangle face framed by that thick, black hair.

"And you will sit down," Nordin hissed quietly as they got to the table. "If you hurt yourself, I will never let you hear the end of it."

Both women were smiling, so Maddox took that as a good sign. An emotional breakthrough of some sort, from the hard, quiet woman he had first met.

She sat. Nordin withdrew and disappeared. Maddox sat

across from her, keeping a neutral smile as Vanya Dowe stood in a corner and pretended that she was a steward serving them tonight. If *Doctor Kay* had carried powered boarding armor, Dowe would have worn it, but they'd never been issued any.

"Commander," Hajós said with a quiet smile. "Am I in trouble?"

"On the contrary," Maddox countered. "I figured that you'd appreciate getting out of the medbay and moving around. We're a few days from completing the current mission, so I thought it would be a good time to ask what you needed."

Reticence. He saw that in her eyes. An unwillingness to talk to strangers. Freya Vilchis had suggested that as a potential cultural cue, based on Metra's history with *Copez*.

"Walk to the bottom of the gangplank and vanish?" she asked carefully.

"If you desire," he nodded. "You have the cash, currently locked up in my safe but you'll get it back when you want. In fact, I'll deliver it tonight after dinner, since I have your papers, too. If Astarte III, I can recommend a few places to stay. And introduce you to some folks, as the woman who practically owns the colony considers us a friend."

"Your lover?" Hajós asked, eyeing him sharply.

He wondered what rumors she'd heard from Doc or someone. Or if he'd let a little too much into his voice when mentioning Asya. Or asked a crew member about Astarte III. Something.

"We have been intimate a few times," he replied. "But she's her own woman. And one of the most dangerous ones I've ever met. Fellow travelers who occasionally enjoy an evening together might better describe it. But this is about you, not me. What do you need to complete your mission?"

Again, the words somewhat surprised him, but Maddox let his unconscious mind pick them. And they were correct, because she had a flinch she was unable to suppress fast enough.

"My mission?" she asked, unconvincingly.

Maddox watched her, practically smelling Vanya Dowe ramp up her focus a level from the corner as she picked up a water pitcher and moved to the table. Filling glasses, and close enough to use it as a weapon.

If Perry was correct, Maddox didn't think Dowe was good enough to take her, but he also didn't doubt that Perry and a few of his people were just outside the hatch, watching on a monitor.

"Your mission," Maddox repeated. "You are a long ways from home. Traveling alone in hostile territory. Jaffa's World isn't the sort of place tourists frequent. Ergo, you had a specific reason for going there. A purpose. A mission, if you will."

Dowe finished filling glasses and stepped back to the corner. Food would be next, but Maddox hoped that they would hold off for a bit while the tension was amped up.

"Earlier, you suggested that you might help?" Hajós asked in a sideways kind of voice. "What shape might that take?"

"What did you need?" Maddox countered. "We're headed to Astarte III for lack of a better destination currently, but if you had coordinates that would be preferable, I'd be happy to entertain them. We are Survey Corps, so going new places is literally in the job description."

He sat back and watched. Hajós watched him back, indecisive.

He turned to Dowe and nodded. Probably time to go ahead and eat, since it looked like Hajós would keep her secrets.

Then she surprised him.

"There is a place," she offered quietly. "I was pursuing details when I got..."

"Ambushed?" he offered.

"Yes, ambushed," she agreed.

"Where is this place?" he asked, making a private bet with himself that she wouldn't tell him.

A woman of mystery, intent on keeping her own counsel.

He could honor that. It gave her back agency that he'd taken away.

She watched. Dowe went ahead and opened a window and pulled through a covered bowl of food, delivering it to the center of the table, then going back for three more.

Maddox had worked it out with Grippen. Communal bowls, so nobody was poisoning her. Shitty way to look at the galaxy, but something Vilchis had said had suggested it, and it *felt* right.

Meat in a brown sauce. Rice steamed. Frozen vegetables, also steamed. Basic stuff that Nordin had approved, once she felt that Hajós could digest solid food, having let the drugs heal her innards.

He took the spoon and filled his plate, then handed it to her, working through everything. She matched him, watching. No wine tonight, because it would mess with the drugs in Hajós's system.

They ate in relative silence. He was fine with that. She would tell him, or she wouldn't, and she could walk off his deck in a week and vanish into legend with this crew.

They had done their duty, and that was as high an acknowledgment as he could think of.

"I don't know where they live," Hajós said abruptly, as plates got cleared for a dessert pastry. "I was hunting them and know they had dealings with folks in Jaffa's World. I didn't get far there."

"Who?" Maddox asked.

"Bandits," she replied finally, leaving him hanging for a long beat. "Pirates, I suppose you might call them."

As before, she could taste Dowe's energy fill the room. Hajós did as well, because she turned and studied the woman. Then turned back to him.

"We've had some dealings with pirates," he offered.

"Oh?"

Maddox skipped over the parts about how he came to be in command of this vessel, instead more or less starting with that distress call from *Livingston* that eventually led him on to Astarte III and those pirate/smugglers, then off to *Wandering Hurricane*, the pirate that had attacked a freighter close to where *Doctor Kay* had been placing the first of those special Science Station™ probes that were watching pirates sail into a nearby harbor.

"So this Astarte III might be a place with a piracy problem?" she asked when he finished.

"Not officially," he replied carefully. "It has a quieter reputation. But yes, it is not as pristine as one might suspect."

"I seek something," Hajós said, voice suddenly shifting. From quiet to steel, maybe. "It was stolen. I have sworn to recover it."

"Pirates have it?" he asked, a little unable to contain his own tones.

Fleet was in the process of dropping a sledgehammer of a patrol squadron on that first pirate base he'd found. A whole mess of frigates, probably with a light cruiser as a flag vessel. You wanted a lot of small guns that could damage pirate ships before they could run, rather than a line of battle that could pound on another one.

And he'd been specifically—publicly—ordered to be elsewhere during this operation, so folks didn't think *Doctor Kay* was involved. Smart ones probably suspected, but smart ones became smugglers instead of pirates anyway. Easier to maintain. Probably more profitable.

Less likely to have the hounds of hell drop out of Ghost-space on your harbor and blow up your fleet.

Hajós studied him. Turned and specifically studied Dowe. Maddox had intentionally selected Vanya Dowe to handle this duty tonight, being female. He didn't know if it mattered to the stranger, but he didn't know that it didn't, either.

Hajós seemed to think so.

"It was stolen from the head of my clan," she finally said. "The thief carried it away, but was on a ship taken by pirates and killed, as near as I have been able to tell. They might have kept it, but they probably sold it on as loot. Hints had pointed me to Jaffa's World. How far away is Astarte III?"

"Not that far, as interstellar distances go," Maddox replied. "A week's hard sail. Two weeks if you relax about it. We were running a circuit to handle probes, and will loop back. Astarte might be a good place to fence loot like that."

"Your helicopter," she nodded.

Okay, so she'd definitely been talking to Doc Nordin about more than health issues. Probably asking hard questions because a woman alone and functionally kidnapped, with a woman medic willing to answer. And those two had seemingly gotten over stiffness.

But yeah, a helicopter.

He hadn't actually ridden in it in that configuration yet, but it worked well as a boat and a land vehicle. The engineering staff aft had all gotten a little nuts on the project, once they had the generator in hand and no reason to give it back.

"Correct," he said anyway. "Would you allow assistance in seeking this—whatever it is?" he asked her, point blank.

She got cagey. Closed up. Focused.

Maddox nodded at the way he was kind of forcing himself into her world, but only if she wanted help. She could walk to the bottom of the gangplank and vanish. Or not.

It was up to her to decide.

"What kind of assistance?" she finally asked.

"We have certain connections in Hithadhel Port," he offered. "Unofficial, as it were. Places we could make inquiries for you."

"What if the clues took me elsewhere?" Hajós asked.

"If it involved hunting pirates, I might be able to convince my bosses to let me go," he replied, already knowing that a message like that would immediately be sent on to Mariami Gelashvili, Permanent First Secretary (Civil Service): *A'Zedi* Intelligence Operations.

The only woman he knew who was dangerous enough to be in a class with Asya Orlova, the Sabine Star herself.

Maddox did put a question mark next to Toshiko Hajós, though, at least in his head.

"They would do that?" she pressed.

"Part of this mission we're on right now involves setting up listening posts that might help us find the pirates who operated *Wandering Hurricane,*" he said, knowing that he was dancing on the edge of telling a civilian too much, but letting his subconscious mind guide him. "It's probably too much to ask that they're also your pirates, but fewer pirates—less piracy—is a good thing, however we get there."

Her blink was a joy to behold. Actual surprise, which he

didn't think he'd done to the woman up until now. He held himself perfectly still. Dowe did as well.

Finally, Hajós held out a hand and Maddox took it in a strong grip.

He wasn't sure what sort of partnership they were creating, but it would be good.

FIFTEEN

Expert Sailor Adrian Stevens wasn't entirely certain how she'd gotten herself into this situation, as she worked her way down quiet side streets in Hithadhel. Somewhere behind her, Serge was a ghost, pacing her and keeping her safe, not that she worried too much around here.

Rough place, sure, but nowhere near the top ten trouble spots she'd gotten herself into.

And out of.

Still, it had to say something weird when she'd been *ordered* to do her black marketeering. Official cover and all that silliness.

Civilian attire today. Ship crew, but not military. Some nobody off the docks.

Ship was on the land reservation instead of parked in the water. Easier to get around, since it didn't involve a boat that everyone in the harbor would notice.

Finally, she got where she was going. Landside entrance to Arkez Machinery, after a double loop to watch for tails and set

Broom up to watch her. Nobody, but that just meant that they were good enough to not be seen.

If they existed.

She entered. Same mechanical bell over the door. Same open space up front with some chairs and a side table holding old magazines. Counter across the room, dividing, with all the important stuff in back, where you asked someone politely for it and they looked the part number up.

One sleepy-looking, grumpy-looking old man resting his ass on a stool, watching her approach with wary eyes. Pale skin so much lighter than hers. *Wronlori* skin colors. Light brown hair gone gray gone silver gone white.

"Hey, kid," Phoward said.

Phoward Arkez, Owner, Arkez Machinery. A nice cover for smuggling and fencing. He'd gotten her the generator last time around. No questions asked.

"Hey," she replied, stepping up so she could talk quietly. "All good around here?"

"Nothing ever changes," he nodded, glancing back over her shoulder, but they were alone in here, unless there were cops hiding in back to entrap her. "What brings you in?"

"Hunting a rumor," Adrian replied. "A memory of a thing. Memorable. Stolen, far as I can tell. Owner's paying a reward for return."

She wasn't, at least as far as Adrian knew, but she also figured that Nevin might post some reward money if they ended up smashing another pirate ring around here. Or Fleet would, which would be even better.

Someone, anyway, and a little of that could stick to Adrian's fingers going by.

"What kind of thing?" Phoward asked, eyes boring in.

Adrian had had to interview Toshiko Hajós, and dig pretty deep to get it straight. Still weirded her out a little.

"Necklace," she replied. "String of blood red pearls. Broach that contains a natural blue diamond set in iridium, laser etched inside with two faces, woman and man."

The woman was more important, but Adrian agreed. Teodora Kardos, original Founder of the *Amaechi Concordancy*, and her husband Frigyes.

"Blue diamond?" he asked.

"Dunno if natural or grown," Adrian shrugged. "Pearls supposedly naturally that color, though."

"Spendy," he nodded. "How far from home is it?"

As in, was it something locally known that would need to be broken up and sold in pieces, or so distant that nobody would recognize it? There was a fine line in fencing stolen goods.

"Most of civilized space," Adrian told him, without mentioning directions.

Astarte III was in an upper, right-hand corner on most traditional maps of the four nations. Metra was in the middle of the left edge.

Phoward nodded sagely.

"Reward for return?" he confirmed to her own nod. "Nothing I've seen or heard about, but I don't generally deal with jewelry."

"Know that," Adrian replied. "Figured I'd start with you and pay a finder's fee for information if you dug any up. Or you earned points with your connections for introducing me on."

There were rules to the game. Favors that went back and forth. Patience got you farther than money. Politeness opened doors that would otherwise remain locked.

Phoward smiled compactly, acknowledging the debts involved, but he'd played straight with her the times they'd done business. And he had a good rep in this region of space.

If you knew how to ask.

"Reach you at your ship?" he inquired.

"Commander's taking a couple weeks to give crew leave," she replied. "We kinda got chased out of Jaffa's World in a hurry."

"Surprised nobody got killed, if you went there," he laughed harshly. "I only send ex-bouncers or special operations troopers, if I need to deal with those yahoos."

"Boss is a hardass that way," she lied. Nobody here could catch her out on it. "Offered to open fire into the crowd with ship's guns if they gave him any grief."

Which was technically true. The best kind of truth.

Phoward shuddered, though. Message received that Knight Nevin knew how to play hardball when he had to. Adrian had only gotten tidbits about how Captain Boru on *Marrakesh* had been kidnapped, and Nevin had led the team that shot their way in and saved the man.

Worse, Nevin had been the one to specifically order Adrian into action today, instead of doing it any other way.

Man was too smart and too subtle for her comfort. Dangerous combination in a commanding officer.

She figured that she could get herself into a lot of trouble.

"Chat soon," he said.

Adrian took that as a dismissal and bailed. Out and down the street to a coffee shop she'd taken a shine to on the last couple of visits. Serge Broom managed to be exactly in front of her in line, but they didn't acknowledge one another.

His way of telling her she was safe.

For now.

SIXTEEN

Toshiko knew that Lise meant well. And approached her medicine with the seriousness of a warrior. The wound might have been fatal for any number of reasons, but Lise—and Nevin—had saved her life. Had allowed her to continue her mission.

To bring an end to the dishonor that had been inflicted upon her clan.

She was up and about these days. The tall man had paid attention to her training, as had many of his team. All bore the marks of close combat training, but not the sorts she did.

They were brawlers, not samurai. Or onna-musha. Not like Toshiko, although Perry came closest.

She hadn't asked for her sword back, and they had not offered, so she focused on open hand forms for now, starting extremely soft and fluid and working only slowly up to iron shirt rigidity. Step. Block. Strike. Step. Grapple. Block. Strike.

The forms looked like dance, and it had been some time since she had approached them with such softness. Usually she was one to step in and execute a damaging blow.

But she was still healing, and the muscles complained when she flexed too hard. Or twisted.

Still, Toshiko pushed. She had been in bed far longer than she would have allowed herself if not for Lise. Kin might have accused her of laziness, had they seen her.

Toshiko was cognizant of the warriors perking up as she worked in the main space. The Medbay was large enough to do her forms, if she compacted everything down into a single mat on the floor, as was traditional. Today, she had chosen to move to the common area, where there was open floor for this sort of training, surrounded by tables, couches, and chairs for crew to relax or work.

The ship was open to local atmosphere. A storm front had begun rolling in and it would rain in a few hours, but for now, the air was simply charged with potential.

As was she.

One of the female warriors approached as she completed a kata. They had obviously seen her do it enough times to know the pattern, because both women came to rest almost identically.

Toshiko studied her. Specialist Trinity Diseth. Young. Oh, so young. Wiry and short. Dark skin and dark brown hair.

"It is permitted to learn the form?" Diseth asked politely.

Toshiko considered the words. They had to have video of her doing it. Perhaps several such, from different angles, where a proper student could learn the basics.

There was still something to having a teacher correcting you in real time.

This crew had given her space respectfully. Treated her as one of them, but courteously, when she had unconsciously been expecting some level of surliness. Churlishness.

But they were not *Copez*. She had to stop and remember

that. *A'Zedi* was a different culture. Much younger the other major nations. They had an openness that she found refreshing and bewildering.

Knight Nevin had stepped into battle because he had thought she needed help, facing five-to-one odds. And he had apologized for that presumption, but someone had shot her in the stomach, and that would have been the death of her on Jaffa's World.

The end of her quest. Endless dishonor.

Toshiko bowed to the woman.

"How much do you know?" she asked.

"Some," Diseth replied, returning the bow.

"Show me," Toshiko ordered, falling into the starting stance next to her and beginning.

Diseth had been watching video. That much was obvious. Hands and feet were close enough for a new student. Body turns and stance were subtly wrong, but only subtly.

But then, as a warrior, it would be expected for the woman to have some knowledge. Adn there were only so many ways for the human body to move.

Diseth was a white belt in these forms. She was not a white belt.

And had asked to learn.

It was another way of belonging.

Toshiko nearly faltered at that thought. How long had it been since she had *belonged*?

Years on the quest, tracing after Luthien's Amulet, once it had been stolen. Slow, patient years, sniffing like a hound after any memory, until she had found the culprit.

Others had derided her for monomaniacal devotion, but to Toshiko, it was merely honor.

You believed in it, or you did not. There was no middle ground. No *good enough*.

It had driven her most of the way across known space. And nearly gotten her killed.

They completed the form. Diseth obviously felt comfortable enough to stand on a dojo floor with it as a student.

"Again," Toshiko ordered, turning to watch. "Slowly."

This time, she moved in and corrected. Hands. Feet. Hips. Head. Not much. The woman had the basics, and this kata was one that only took days to learn.

Lifetimes to master.

Others were watching. Quietly. Corners of eyes. Toshiko wondered how many might stand up if she announced a training class. And if she wanted to.

These people were warriors. And understood honor, at least enough to charge into a fight against uneven odds.

The Holy Fathers would never risk injury thus. Someone might ruin their fancy silks with blood or spilled wine.

Nevin had allowed her to bleed all over himself, personally carrying her to safety.

She bowed to Trinity when the woman completed.

"It is a beginning," she said. "Now, I think Lise expects me to rest. You continue practicing."

Trinity bowed to her, as a student did a teacher. Others smiled.

Toshiko retreated to the medbay. She needed rest, yes.

More importantly, she needed time to think.

SEVENTEEN

Narayana was in the map room. Maddox had established the pattern, and made it acceptable for the enlisted crew to largely manage themselves on the bridge. Several had flourished as a result, so Narayana had extended it.

Adrian Stevens appeared at the hatch, dressed as a civilian, because Maddox had ordered her out of uniform most of the time the ship was on the ground on this trip. Narayana still laughed at the occasional bewilderment that action had inflicted on Stevens.

She had always been dancing on the edge of trouble with her black marketeering. Now she was indulging herself.

Narayana smiled to prompt her.

"I have a lead," she said simply.

Narayana jolted like someone had grounded a lightning bolt through his chair.

"Where?"

"Here," she replied. "Not all that recently, but not that long ago, as these things go."

Narayana pointed to the other chair.

"Talk."

"Toshiko said that a thief had taken it," Stevens said as she planted her butt. "Then got taken by what we presume were pirates. Since the ship is kinda in the pirate-hunting business quietly these days, I studied some of the flow patterns and identified three possible river channels."

Narayana paused and considered her language. Her implications.

He's never crossed over that line, and these days stayed as close to regulations and expectations as he possibly could, understanding that his next mistake ended his career for good.

But, river channels? A delta of stolen goods? Made sense.

"How many of them end up on Astarte III?" he asked, dreading the answer.

"Only one," she nodded. "However, given circumstances, possibly the biggest one, because the alternatives take you directly into *A'Zedi* from the north-northwest, or out into *Unaffiliated Space* coreward."

"And Astarte III?"

"Lateral, with a soft connection back to *A'Zedi* on a quieter smuggling frontier, plus you can continue and fork to either keep going straight where you end up in *Wronlori*, or circle clockwise and reach *Traisa*. Both of those are more likely, if you keep the item intact, which brings you a LOT more value than individual pearls and stone. You get history at that point."

"What's the history worth?" Narayana asked, intrigued.

"Tack two zeroes on," Stevens smiled grimly. "Maybe four, depending."

Narayana whistled.

"So you followed your instincts and it landed here at some point?" he pressed.

"Affirmative, sir," Stevens said. "Weirdly, it turned up in a poker game."

"Poker?"

"Card games, played for high stakes by professional players," she explained.

Narayana was vaguely familiar, but given his druthers, he'd have a mug of spiked hot chocolate and a backgammon game. Or a good book.

"What happened?" he asked, feeling the ground open up beneath his feet and threaten to swallow him whole into criminality.

"Somebody went all in on an inside straight," she grinned. "Faceplanted on four deuces."

He assumed that all of those words meant something as a unit. Each made sense. The collection? None.

Stevens caught that.

"Epic game. Epic players," she expanded. "Based on the rumors and laughter still floating around, somebody had to go beyond table stakes when he thought that he had a winning hand and ran out of money. Put up the amulet as collateral in the pot. With me so far?"

Narayana processed that. Maybe. He nodded.

"Others think that he was set up, and the winner had stacked the cards. Or was dealing off the bottom of the deck," she said. "Something. Doesn't really matter. Memory of the amulet was enough. It was present on the planet here six months ago. Before we came through the first time. Most recent time."

The ship had been through several years ago. An early sailing under Kumar Das. Not since, until Maddox had brought them here, hunting pirates.

"Do we know who the losing party was?" he asked.

"Rumors suggest a pirate of some sort," she smiled broadly. "One of those occasional businessmen with excess cargo to sell cheap, as long as you don't ask which truck it fell off of."

Narayana nodded. He knew that type. They'd bought the generator as a way of proving stolen and smuggled goods. That had led them to at least one pirate base so far.

"This guy related to either of the clans of punks we're stalking?" he asked.

"Negative," she stated flatly, that smile gone hard. "Think there's a third bunch. Or branch office."

"Could you map your river channels, running from *Copez* to *Astarte*?" he asked, automatically reaching for the master map binder.

Sure, it was easier to bring it all up electronically, but he was a little old-fashioned that way. And having the binders meant that you could touch things. Smell them while researching, which helped imprint it better on his mind.

"Sir?" Stevens asked, thoroughly confused now.

"We might be forward homeported here," he told her. "There is, however, no reason not to expand our little network of science stations, if we knew where to look."

"Game trails," she said, suddenly seeing it. "Sure, I can think of a couple of places where you might plant listeners, if you wanted to look for folks hiding from the authorities. Might not be pirates, though."

"Granted," he replied. "*Unaffiliated* worlds are independent for a reason. But I think we'd likely earn another gold star if we could overlay known *Unaffiliated* worlds against newly colonized places. Or spots suddenly busy with unexplainable traffic."

"Like smugglers congregating," she said. "Or pirates establishing a new base to raid from."

"Exactly, Stevens," he said. "I care less about smugglers, except as they allow piracy to flourish, but if we crush pirates entirely, then we save a lot of people from being taken. Or killed. Galaxy is big enough for folks who want to sail off and *Unaffiliate* themselves, as long as they don't hurt folks."

He paused as she digested that. For a woman who liked to color outside the lines, he had rudely pulled her back onto the side of law and order.

"What about the amulet?" he asked.

"Tracking the gambler now," she said. "High stakes games, so I came into the rumors dockside, but nobody I've been able to talk to was in the room."

"Who was?" he asked.

"Sir?"

"What socio-economic status was around the table?" Narayana turned formal.

"Oh," she breathed. "Upper middle and lower upper, sir. Couple might have been lower class in fancy duds putting on airs, but you need money to get in that room, so only a few pretenders. Professional gamblers are good at appearing nice and wholesome, but usually originate from the bottom of the pyramid, then get ahead on work ethic and a touch of sociopathic behavior."

Narayana nodded. Work your ass off, and don't really care who you hurt in the process of getting ahead. Anti-social behavior, but places like Astarte III existed outside the rules of *A'Zedi* or *Wronlori*. They made their own rules.

"What can the rest of us do to help your search?" he asked.

Stevens paused. He could see her hemming and hawing. Trying to decide how much to reveal. How much to hide, lest it get her in trouble.

"I only care about the gambler," he reinforced. "And then, only to track the amulet. Would he have kept it?"

"Doubtful, sir," she perked up. "Likely sold it on. Or lost it in another game. Maybe gave it to a saloon girl, if he thought it was fake."

"Or so valuable that someone might come after him with a sword?" he asked.

She suddenly leaned back, remembering how this crazy mission had come about.

"Yeah, maybe," she said quietly. "Better if you got value out of it immediately, then kept moving, like a shark."

"Excellent work, Stevens," he said. "You keep hunting. And bring in folks if you need. Then draw me your map in your spare time, so I can go to the Knight with it."

"Aye, sir."

Then he was alone. Brooding, but mostly redrawing certain assumptions. How did they track that gambler?

And where?

EIGHTEEN

Maddox listened to the explanation from Yadav. Heard all of it. Digested it. He knew Adrian Stevens as a crew member with illicit ties.

Nothing had prepared him for the scale.

They were in his office forward, instead of the map room. Crew was largely standing down and rotating shifts for leave into town. Vessel had undergone all the maintenance it needed at present.

Everyone was relaxed.

"You think we should kidnap a man, even though you're reasonably certain that he does not have the item in question?" Maddox confirmed.

They'd been in Hithadhel Port for a week. Apparently, it had been long enough for Stevens to completely rip the cover off smuggling in this town.

Or it was worse than he'd imagined.

Or the crew trusted him that much.

Maddox wasn't sure which answer was the least unsettling.

"I agree with Stevens's assessment that he's unlikely to still have it on his person," Narayana replied. "Her logic holds, as far as I can follow it. And he'd unlikely to talk unless he's in an uncomfortable situation."

"What's to keep him from lying?" Maddox asked. "From spinning up a fanciful yarn of utter bullshit designed to send us down the wrong track?"

"Keeping him hostage," Narayana replied with a grimness that chilled the air. "It allows threats that he might not make it home safe if we don't get what we want."

"Are we planning extra-judicial punishments?" Maddox asked, drawing a seriously hard line in the sand.

Narayana Yadav's sudden smile was probably worse.

"Absolutely not," he laughed. "However, I'm pretty sure there are warrants out for his arrest in *A'Zedi* space, though. Or bounties for capture. Even the threat thereof should jar him into motion. We don't want him. We want who the amulet went to."

"And nobody will tell you where to find him?" Maddox asked.

"We haven't asked," the man replied, sobering again. "Stevens assures me that us trying to locate him by asking the underworld causes him to immediately jump on a ship if he's still on planet, running like hell for the darkness and we'll be years tracking him down."

"Like Hajós has been?" he asked.

"Exactly like that, yes," Narayana agreed. "I'm told that this requires subtlety. That's where you come in."

Maddox didn't bother not rolling his eyes at that comment. He'd been accused of a lot of things in his career. *Nuance* was not generally one of them.

Still, he could learn. Captain Boru had always said that you had to spend your life learning, because there was always something new.

"What am I doing?" he asked.

"Inviting the Sabine Star to dinner," Narayana replied. "Private room at Bistro Himilco. I've inquired and Chef Hysmith loves you enough to tell us whenever you needed such a thing."

Maddox grunted noncommittally. Damned amazing food, because Scott Hysmith was a fantastic chef. One of the main reasons Maddox had been in favor of stationing out of Astarte III, as a matter of fact.

"And she'll tell me?" he pressed. "She knows?"

"I doubt it," Narayana nodded. "She does, however, have the resources to find him, in ways we never could."

"And she'll do this for us, just like that?" Maddox asked.

"I'm sure you'll find a way to charm her, boss," Narayana leered.

Another eye roll seemed appropriate.

"Plus, I think we should introduce her to Hajós at some point," Narayana turned serious again. "I feel like those two women would bond on a level most of us hardly ever achieve."

Maddox could see that. He'd spent enough time around the newcomer to see the charisma she had. The effect on his crew. And he knew Asya could dominate any room.

It would be a match made in heaven or hell. No middle ground there.

Still, geas, and all that such a thing implied.

And Asya did appear to like him. Respect him, even, understanding that they had two, separate lives that could intersect from time to time without him making any demands on her.

Because she owned this world. Possibly literally, though

he'd never inquired. Certain things he figured he was better off not knowing.

"I did tell you to handle it," Maddox finally said. "So I can't exactly bitch about you doing exactly that. What do you need?"

"You to call her and make the invite," Narayana said. "I'll work with her staff for everything else."

Maddox nodded. Then paused as he had a thought.

"Yes?" Narayana asked, suddenly a touch nervous.

"The necklace," Maddox said, waiting for a nod. "Whoever has it. Do they know what it is?"

"Probably not, this far from home," Narayana offered. "Might just be a pretty artifact to them. I would expect a real collector to be *A'Zedi* or *Traisa*. Maybe *Wronlori*, but that doesn't feel right."

"And when we track it down, you were just planning on letting Hajós kill whoever had it and take it back?"

It was obvious that Narayana hadn't gotten that far in his planning. Too busy with the trees to see the forest, as it were.

Maddox nodded and keyed the intercom.

"Hull office," Repair Officer Squire Astrid Calder replied.

"Calder, it's Knight Nevin," he said. "I'm forward in my office. Are you available to join me?"

He could order it, but she might be doing something more important than talking to him. None of this had to happen today.

"Be right there, sir," she said, and cut the line.

Narayana opened the hatch and shifted to the other chair. It was crowded in here with three, but he didn't feel like moving to the map room.

Squire Calder appeared quickly. Repair Officer, answering to Joy Kimmel as Shipfitter. *Ms. Fixit* was her other nickname.

A pretty woman, when she wasn't covered in dirt or grease, with lighter brown hair than a lot of the crew and a long nose that balanced wideset eyes.

It was her hobby in her spare time that he needed right now.

"Sir?"

"Sit," he pointed. "I have a project for you to undertake, as part of your commanding officer's eccentricities, Calder."

She moved warily. The crew had gotten to know him over the past few months, but there were still dark spots in places. Might be traps, but might just be gaps.

He smiled to put her at ease.

"Our guest," he began, framing things for her.

"Toshiko, yes," Calder nodded.

Maddox paused and noted that a lot of folks referred to Hajós by her first name. He hadn't moved to that level of informality, but might.

"She's hunting a thing," Maddox said.

"The amulet."

"The amulet, yes," Maddox agreed. "I'd like you to talk to her. Get a really good description of it. Then build me a replacement."

Both of them were confused.

"Sir?" Calder asked.

"When we find it, we might swap whoever has it at that point," Maddox said. "Stolen goods, but far outside jurisdiction. If they had a replacement, they might not squawk as much. Talk to...Toshiko. Ask her for details. I understand blood red pearls, a platinum base, and a blue diamond with two faces etched inside. I presume we could replicate that, if someone wanted *pretty* as opposed to literal. Have her ask me if she has questions, but this might be how it ends, when we track it down. Deck Officer here can handle most things otherwise. Questions?"

"Ship's resources?" Calder asked.

"If we have it, use it," Maddox decided. "If not, ask the Deck Officer about acquiring it. Expert Sailor Stevens can probably handle that part, but I don't know what the budget would need to be."

He speared Narayana with a specific look.

"We've got a budget for bribes that can probably be stretched pretty far here," Maddox said simply.

Let the Deck Officer handle it. His job.

Maddox was likely to have his hands full, if he was standing exactly between Toshiko and Asya.

Anybody would.

NINETEEN

Maddox had enjoyed dinner. First rate meal, in the company of an amazingly beautiful woman who knew some seriously funny dirty jokes. Hysmith had outdone himself with the seafood steaks. And the vegetables. And the rolls.

Dessert was a thing of chocolates, pastry, cream filling, and utter goodness that they shared from a single plate in the middle.

Between bites, she suddenly locked hard on him.

"To what do I owe all this?" she asked, voice a slow-burn drawl that he'd happily listen to reading accounting records.

"Lots of things," Maddox replied. "Some good. Some serious."

"Serious?"

He knew better than to try to lie or dissemble around the woman. Too smart. Too capable. Too dangerous. In good ways, too.

"Partly, I get to be collateral damage when I asked Hysmith to make something amazing for a special event," Maddox smiled. "Partly, I wanted to ask your help for something, and figured that this was better than coffee in your office. Bribing you, as it were."

"Oh?"

She hadn't gone cold, but had developed a level of reserve. Not as much as normal, if they were meeting in public, but not as seducible, were he headed that direction.

He nodded. Turned serious himself.

"On Jaffa's World, we ran into a situation," he said, then proceeded to give her a high-level rundown of his last three weeks. "From there, my people think the person in question is still on Astarte III, but haven't looked too hard for fear of spooking him."

"And what are you asking from me?" she pressed, all business now, though there was still a little dessert left for her to keep digging into with a spoon.

"This is your world, Asya," he reminded her. "The rest of us are all guests here, including me and mine. Anything we do here is because you allow it."

That surprised her. Good surprise, he thought, but surprise, nonetheless.

He wondered how many men would automatically assume that a woman was in charge. Should be in charge. Didn't challenge her on the topic.

She recovered after a moment. Softened a little.

"What I'd like is your help quietly finding the man," Maddox continued. "Mostly, finding the amulet, but we have to either find him or find out where it might have gone from him. He might be on planet, since this appears to be his base of operations, but he might have left. We'd like to find him. Capture him, because my people assure me that just asking won't do any good, so they want control."

"And when you're done with him?" Asya asked.

"I presume we can turn him loose," Maddox replied. "Though if he turns out to be more dangerous or wanted than a mere gambler, we might haul him home. Or ask you. I doubt he needs official sanctioning, but my people know he deals with pirates, so I'm reserving judgment. I'd like your permission. And your help."

She started to say something, but caught herself. Studied him closely.

Small woman. *Wronlori* coloration, so pale skin that only barely tanned to a golden brown. Dark blue eyes that were so bright. Brown hair up in a bun with chopsticks holding it.

Utterly gorgeous, on top of everything else.

But Maddox understood that he had walked up to a line that might change their relationship from whatever it had been to something else. Wherever that went.

"I want to meet this woman," she said simply.

Maddox nodded. He'd expected that.

"And you said that you had a jeweler in your crew making a copy of the necklace?" she continued.

"Not exact, but a close replica, assuming we might be able to trade someone who didn't know what it was," he replied. "Or particularly care."

"Make two copies," she ordered.

She could do that. It was her world. Her government. Her everything. If he wanted her help, he'd have to do it her way.

Maddox nodded.

She finished the last bite of the small chocolate mountain. Smiled at him.

"I have other questions, but this isn't the place to discuss them," she told him.

"Where?" he asked.

"You're coming up for a nightcap," she informed him. "We'll talk more there."

Maddox agreed. He doubted that it would merely be a quick drink then send him on his way, at least from the smile she was giving him, but he'd keep his options open.

TWENTY

Steve Perry wandered into the VLS bays with a question, uncertain who could answer it. Several of them had had a hand in the original creation, but he'd stepped back after that.

Lead Expert Lori Boyce happened to be tinkering, so he approached her and made enough noise for her to look up.

"Am I in trouble?" she asked, wrench still in one grease-covered hand as she looked up from something she was repairing.

"Dunno," he smiled. "Anything you need to confess?"

"Oh, Pretty, we'd be here all week," she laughed.

Steve doubted it. She put on a good show, but Boyce didn't have that crazy, dangerous edge that you got with some pilots.

He walked over and smacked the hull of the vehicle they'd built after the last set of adventures on Astarte III. After all, having bought stolen goods and not wanting to arrest anyone, what else did you do with a generator?

"How big a crew can this handle in flight?" he asked.

Lori rose and walked close.

"What are my mission parameters?" she countered, suddenly lethal.

"Low, fast insertion," Steve said. "Small arms at most, because it's a stealth strike, not a bombardment. Not sure the best way to insert a team, but airborne feels the fastest."

"Me piloting," she nodded. "You and up to four others, if you're not bringing anything but basic packs and armored vests. Low is a relative term, because I need space to stay clear of the rotors when landing, so you'll need a clearing or parking lot. Folks in the bed need to stay down and hold on tight, if I leave off the shell. I'll be in the cab with someone, presumably you?"

"Dunno," Steve shrugged. "This is when we find the guy we're after. Might be able to sneak up on him, but likely only one person, so Serge or Sankar. Rest of the team needs to land like a hammer."

"*Packrat* is faster and carries more gear," she said. "*Nevin's Folly* is quiet."

"Whatever you do, change the name to something else," Perry ordered quietly. "Immediately. That was funny at first, but it shows a level of disrespect for your commanding officer that is entirely inappropriate. Especially considering what that thing got us. And might do next. Am I clear?"

"Aye, sir," she replied, sobering sharply. "Does is need a simple alphanumeric?"

"It needs something else," Steve told her. "At least polite. Preferably neutral. An inside joke is acceptable."

"We could call it *Selkie*, sir," she offered.

"Selkie?"

"A mythological creature that can shapeshift between seal and human forms by putting on or removing its seal skin," she said, "Legend says that they can be friendly and helpful to humans, but they can also be dangerous and vengeful. Dual nature is kind of appropriate here. As is shapeshifting, all things considered."

"Send me an encyclopedia reference to look up," Steve decided. "We'll go from there. For now, I want you breaking it out, assembling it, and doing some flight testing, with and without folks in the bed. I think you're better off with the shell, and we might carry a smaller team."

"Can do," Boyce nodded. "Immediately?"

"Yes, immediately," Steve ordered. "I have no idea when you'll get the call to fly someone somewhere, so I want you ready to go at the drop of a hat, even if that means you don't get leave time in town."

She was a bit put out by that, but she also was their primary pilot for small craft. Still, he could see maybe cross-training Kellogg at some point to give Boyce time off. That one had the right instincts.

Tomorrow's problem.

Today, he had to figure out how to pounce on someone when they thought they were getting away from him.

And take them alive.

PART 3
GAMBLER

Serge Broom usually drew the short straw when Pretty needed a ghost in town. He had one of those faces that let him vanish into a crowd. Hithadhel always felt bigger than it really was, but that was because the town was so compact. Everyone down on the water's edge in as little space as could be arranged, dominated by the monstrous campus that was the Sabine Star.

Today, he was on a stalk.

Edge of night, because all the interesting folk tended to sleep away the day like vampires. Came out for dinner, then got serious with things.

Private party. Not a mansion, *per se*. More of a manor house at the edge of the civilized zones of town, where the land started uphill into the ring of dead volcanoes that marked this bay. Rich soil, but rocky and not all that flat, so folks did ranching things instead of growing crops.

Mostly show horses, rather than working ranches, but folks could sell beef and pork to the locals at a huge profit, since there were so many fish to be harvested out of the nearby ocean.

Planet could export fish if they wanted, but that would require more industry on a commercial scale, and a lot more people. Serge had gotten the impression that things were the size that the important people wanted them. Not big enough to compete with *A'Zedi* or *Wronlori* worlds, because the place mostly functioned as a warehousing depot.

A'Zedi merchants shipped things here and dropped them off. *Wronlori* folks bought them and carried them on.

And that had been happening even before the most recent war, though if you wanted to be honest, *A'Zedi* and *Wronlori* had been at war for most of a century, off and on.

Locals provided neutral ground. Trade happened. Nobody mentioned uniforms, and frequently him and the others went into town in civilian mufti specifically for that reason.

Rather than take a car or anything that would leave memories later, he'd set out early this morning on foot and spent the whole day wandering through town.

Meandered. Sight-seeing. Bought a few things of little importance, mostly to have an excuse to go shopping. Eaten at various joints progressively farther from the starport.

Folks had noticed him, but not seen him doing anything suspicious, because he was biding his time.

Had been. Sun was setting finally. Time to get into motion.

Serge studied the neighborhood. Residential transition was somewhere behind him. No more entire streets with shops. Instead, you had a corner bar and a corner bodega. Or a small restaurant. Maybe something else, but mostly these buildings were short towers of flats where folks lived.

And he'd been swimming upstream for the last little while, pretending to be a guy just coming off shift as lots of other folks were headed down to restaurants, casinos, shops, or bordellos to work the evening shift.

The town, as they said, came alive in the dark.

Serge left that behind him and trudged, like a man exhausted from a long day and ready to be home. Play-acting, but a thing he did well, which was why Pretty put him on point for it. Head down. Shoulders hunched some. Hands stuffed in jacket pockets, where he happened to be holding a comm on one side and a Type Three Personal Disruptor in the other.

Not that he was expecting to need either, but better safe than sorry.

Next intersection was when things got interesting. Major lateral roadway, with the farms and stuff generally running on the other side.

Lori Boyce had shown him pictures she'd taken from the air. Looked like these farms had been here first, and the city had expanded out to meet them, running into a ring road that just happened to be marked on the far side by three meter brick walls, no doubt reinforced and protected with all manner of electronic eyes and ears.

Good thing he also had a toolkit and a few other things tucked into a pouch on his thigh.

Serge skipped the bodega on the corner. Walked right by, not looking in because he didn't want those folks having a good description later.

No traffic on the road at the moment. And rich folks often flew in skycars instead of riding, but still got deliveries in heavy vans that needed roads and gates.

No easy way to insert via air anyway. Not without noise.

Maybe he'd ask Perry about a hang glider or something if this shit was going to become normal.

Whatever *normal* was.

Serge walked, head down and focused. Low profile.

Across the street. Up a long roadway that seemed to divide a pair of bigger ranches, at least from the aerial view. Different architecture on either side of the road, with larger stones making up the wall to the left and more brick to the right, like maybe it had been here first and defined everything.

He knew the woman everyone called the Sabine Star lived behind him in town. Up in her loft that the commander visited occasionally. She didn't own this ranch, but Serge didn't know who did. Someone on a first name basis with her, obviously.

Lots of money, which usually meant shipping around here. Also a good place for predators to swarm. Serge didn't do card games. Too easy to cheat. Too easy to run into a professional who knew all sorts of ways to take your money.

He'd stay with drinking and vids for entertainment.

And sneaking up on people.

Darkness had fallen by the time he got to his destination. Just low enough to throw long shadows. End of day tired before evening folks came on duty and got serious.

It was a gate. Ship had taken images of everything while landing. Survey did that. Most vessels didn't store it. Didn't use it to build up extensive and comprehensive maps of places, down to details that often got overlooked.

Their loss.

Serge sidestepped as he got to the little alcove. Turned around and watched backwards for anyone coming up from behind him. Stood perfectly still for five minutes, like a man without a care in the world.

Up until now, all he was guilty of was prowling. Looking suspicious. Hadn't broken any laws, which might not matter, depending on who owned the cops around here, but the Knight had supposedly cleared things with the woman who owned everybody else, so he had a better feeling than usual.

Still, patience. Things inside weren't supposed to ramp up for a while.

In fact, he heard the first lifter approaching from the south, that loud whine of turbines as they rotated to landing mode and started to settle, somewhere beyond the wall. Someone early to the party. Or late getting home to set up. Last minute catering delivery. Something.

Serge waited. The thing landed, then lifted off a minute later, headed back into town.

He let the darkness stretch, then finally pulled a tool from his pouch. Handscanner came out and listened for anything broadcasting a signal.

Silence on all the commercial bands. He pointed it at the gate itself, and picked up a new signal beside him.

Serge nodded. Sounds around the gate probably threw a huge number of false positives, so they had just marked the gate itself with a circuit. Break it and it let out an alarm, somewhere in the main building. Or maybe they had security separated off.

Place wasn't a fortress. Just a big palace for rich folks. Intel suggested a handful of bodyguards at most, as mostly this was an invite-only party Serge was planning to crash.

He followed the scanner and located where the alarm was on the other side of the gate frame, right next to the lock. Commercial model, from the looks.

He pulled out a small portable drill and quietly bored through the wall, letting the feel of things tell him when the wood was giving way to the alarm box.

A light revealed the interior of the alarm box. He switched tools and got a long, hooked prybar inside, like a bent screwdriver. A couple of tugs and he was pretty sure that the power line was separated. He pulled the scanner and nothing showed, so that part had worked.

Quickly, he picked the lock, uncertain as to whether or not the alarm system had any sort of battery backup or checksum that would call for help.

No time like the present.

He opened the gate a crack and listened. Nothing.

Nothing local, at least.

Breaking. Not yet entering.

Nothing.

He entered, walking on eggshells, but nothing jumped out at him. No dogs or anything on the property, as far as anybody knew.

Just darkness.

He started inward.

TWENTY-TWO

Tavish Arleth liked to think he had led something of a charmed life. Up from practically nothing as a child, he was currently being fed and entertained by some of the wealthiest men on the planet. If he was expected to play for his supper later, Tavish could accept that.

Every game had an ante. The good ones, anyway.

All the people who owned a piece of his soul seemed to agree on that point.

Dinner was as exquisite as he'd been expecting from Vasyly Kretov's on-staff chef and crew. They always knew how to feed a mob for a game. And Kretov had brought in a few new victims tonight. Man was exceptional at poker. Almost good enough to make a living at it.

Almost.

Looking at some of the other players, Tavish figured that he could clean them out in about an hour if he was desperate and in a hurry.

But that was defeating the purpose. He'd been wined and dined. His half of the equation was providing entertainment for the new folks. Men like Tobias Castillon and Urus Warwick. And cleaning them out, while making sure that Kretov came close to breaking even.

Not exactly a crooked house. And it wasn't like Kretov would even notice his losses in a game like this. Man spent more on clothing annually.

But appearances had to be kept.

So, he'd dressed in his fancier duds. The nice outfit, including the paisley vest that folks around here seemed to expect. And he'd even made a show of bringing a pistol in a holster under the jacket he'd worn, leaving both by the door with the butler.

It was all a stage show, but Kretov was happy to let Tavish clean out a few folks regularly. Beat the hell out of working for a living, and nobody around here was all that dangerous. At least physically. Plus, none of them knew what he was really about, so they would take him for a mere gambler and stop looking past that.

These men—and woman with Evgeva Zenkova along tonight—were the kind that owned gunmen. Had killers on staff, quietly. Or direct connections with some of the seedier folks that ran the edges of *Wronlori* space.

Not a direct threat. Folks not to piss off at the table, though, lest they send people after you later.

Tavish had finally settled things down enough to spent more time on Astarte III, after a few misunderstandings a while back. Unfortunate luck, running into people who thought they knew how to play, discovering someone that made them look like cheap marks.

Man still held a grudge, but Tavish had managed to generally evade Dante Markell long enough to slip into the shadows.

And it hadn't hurt that *A'Zedi* had started sniffing around here. Couple of pirate ships had already been taken, and the others were generally keeping their distance, lest they be next.

Tavish watched Kretov rise from the dining table.

"Folks, should we move on to the night's entertainment?" he asked the room.

Heavy-set guy. Bald because he shaved the ring. Looked like a granite sphere for a head. Beady eyes. Mouth like a razor slash.

Growls like hungry wolves replied, and everyone moved around the table and headed to the salon, where Kretov kept a permanent gaming room, an octagonal table in green felt because any good game required at least five players but no more than eight. Past that, the number of games you could play got thinner and thinner, and blackjack got dull after a while.

Kretov sat at the top of the table. Tavish moved to left of opposite from the man. Gorbovich, one of the regulars, was across from him, next to Kretov. Castillon ended up on Tavish's right, and Warwick his left, with Madame Zenkova beyond Warwick.

"Rules are table stakes with one buy-in, as always," Kretov told the two newcomers. "Stud poker. We occasionally play until dawn, with breaks every two hours for coffee and snacks. Questions?"

Looking around, Tavish figured that Madame Zenkova was the only other ringer here. Middle-aged pretty like a fine wine, though wine didn't get plastic surgery. Pleasant voice. A bit vague about how she'd come to Astarte III and where her money came from, but he hadn't drawn up the invite list.

Merely been hired, as it were, to provide top-notch gambling for Kretov's guests.

Tavish tossed in the first chip and shuffled the deck.

TWENTY-THREE

Serge had a decent view through an Analytical Probe-Module. Enhanced optics, washed through some software that went beyond mere infrared. Range finder. Target designator, in case he needed to call down artillery on someone. Even a type of laser that could read vibrations off glass and translate them to words via a wired bud in his ear.

He wasn't sitting at the table with them, but wasn't far from doing just that. And had a pretty good idea how the one guy was cheating, but that was because he could shoot footage, pause it, wind it back, and watch cards come off the bottom of the deck.

Just like a couple of expert crew members had suggested you did such a thing.

Nifty. Hell of a lot of manual dexterity. And speed.

Serge made a mental note that the fellow could probably outdraw just about anybody if he had that damned pistol rig on his hip instead of under his jacket.

The others were more money than brains, though the owner of the joint, if that was the man at the head of the table, projected a cloak of malevolence over things, even from the yard through glass. Not a man you'd want to run into in a dark alley.

Serge located his comm and started typing. Easier than speaking aloud, because far less chance of someone hearing. Night had just enough chill that they'd closed up the glass doors he was watching through, but there might be guards that wandered around the grounds for whatever reason.

Quick tactical layout. Players by dress, since he didn't know any names but Arleth. Styles of play, because he wasn't supposed to do anything but watch until it all broke up.

Deck Officer had assumed that folks would be pretty sharp right now. Sleep all day and show up ready to play games of intellect all night, fortified by food and alcohol.

Take them when they're tired. Plus, only one target here, with the rest being innocent bystanders.

If you could stretch the term that far. Serge didn't figure that anybody in the shipping business on this planet was innocent. Too much smuggling. Too many pirates.

Hell, that one woman who managed the bordello was probably the most honest person in town, because she was up front about what she did and how much it was going to cost.

That brought a smile to his face.

Serge settled back with his optics and kept studying the players.

TWENTY-FOUR

Tavish was about a third up from where he'd started. Zenkova was a ringer, but he couldn't tell if Kretov had known it before the woman had shown up tonight, or if he'd invited her for other reasons. Boobs or money. Tavish didn't care. She had both. And knew how to use them effectively on the other players around the table.

He doubted that she'd have any interest in consummating any of the subtle innuendos she'd left...dangling out there, but he also wasn't about to pursue them. Dangerous woman. Like trying to fuck a wild cat, hoping she didn't rip your belly open and start feeding.

Woman had that air about her, but hadn't started revealing it for the first couple of hours.

In his guise as a random player invited to the table, Tavish couldn't ask Kretov anything useful. He'd worry about that tomorrow. Or not. Maybe that man would draw the losing hand and get saddled with Zenkova when she got hungry.

Tavish figured that he could outrun her, if push came to shove.

Warwick was about out of the game, having had a run of bad luck stacked with bad bluffs. Gorbovich was a bit ahead. Castillon, about even.

Tavish had done this with Kretov enough times to have a feel for the man's timing. He raked in the latest pot a little more slowly than usual.

"This sounds like a good time for a break," Kretov announced. "Smokes, whiskey, and such. Twenty minutes?"

The others nodded, grunted, whatevered. Tavish slid his chair back and stood up slowly, watching the others for tells. Physical ailments that might make them lose focus.

Proper gamblers had to be ready to sit for hours at a table, so he did yoga and other things to keep as flexible as he could. Never knew when that sort of thing might come in handy.

Night had a hint of chill, but Tavish was a little tired of the bad mix of colognes and perfumes in the room, so he took a snifter of brandy and walked out onto the back porch, upwind of Warwick's cigar.

Stars were out. A bit of a breeze. Cool, autumn crispness at this latitude. Lights of Hithadhel below him, spreading out to the water, with just enough elevation from Krekov's place to see most of it.

Warwick tapped out his cigar and nodded, withdrawing back inside. And maybe calling it a night, unless he wanted to buy in a second time and lose twice as much. Only question was how long he wanted to prolong his agony.

Tavish looked around the empty space and nodded to himself. He had a few minutes to himself, and was going to enjoy them.

TWENTY-FIVE

Serge watched the game break up and folks wander around. Didn't feel done, and intel had said they played for several more hours, most of the time, so biobreaks or something. One player emerged and lit a cigar. Target had a glass in one hand and eyes on the stars.

Then Arleth was alone.

Serge typed quickly, knowing that folks were watching.

Target isolated. Orders?

\#\#Watch only for now. No change to timing.\#\#

Serge nodded to himself. Not impossible to get the drop on the man, all of about ten meters away across a few bushes. Any noise, though, and the others might come running. Plus, Pretty wanted him taken later.

He watched. Man over there had fast hands. Nimble. Flexible.

Deadly dangerous, like gamblers in fairy tales were supposed to be.

He settled back to watch.

TWENTY-SIX

Tavish returned to the den of iniquity with a wry smile. His luck had run pretty well lately, after a stretch of about six months where he'd been afraid he was going to have to rent a table from the Sabine Star in town and run an honest game in one of her saloons.

Honest enough, anyway.

Not that it would have been the worst thing, as it would have meant a semi-permanent place to stay. Possibility of accumulating things. Being anchored down when trouble finally found him.

It always did.

He was almost to where he expected things to get to tonight. Outside, about three hours to dawn, so right on schedule. Warwick had tapped out and gone home early. Zenkova had stumbled pretty badly at one point, but that was Tavish deciding that Gorbovich would draw an inside straight on the last card, after tantalizing the man the whole hand.

Kretov was sitting pretty. Tavish had enough cash to live

like a king for a month, if he wanted to take that long off playing.

He'd get bored and start hustling punks with a three-card-monte table long before then. Or take a vacation somewhere where the locals couldn't find him. Meet up with his controller and provide a briefing update on everything happening in the northeast.

Kretov made a show of checking his wristwatch.

"One last hand?" he asked the room.

Tavish didn't care. It was all free money, and he could lose two-thirds of what was in front of him and still come out ahead tonight. On top of the food and entertainment.

And Zenkova had her eyes on Kretov, so he was feeling safe enough.

Tavish nodded and waited for Gorbovich to deal. Man wasn't even a gifted amateur. Merely a sucker happy to pay to be schooled on cards.

But then, every table required a mark or three. People who could lose a big chunk of cash for the ability to rub shoulders with the seedy underbelly of civilization for a time, before returning to their glamorous, sterile lives.

Tavish understood that he provided that to these folks. It was a happy exchange, as far as he was concerned.

Decent hand. Couple of rounds of betting, but nobody had gotten punchy with exhaustion. Nor drawn in four of a kind at the top. Tavish raised a few times, mostly to gig Zenkova into calling and raising him. She had a tell. Thought she could bluff everyone else out of the game and win something big, but was sitting on a weak hand.

Still, better than he had. Not as good as Kretov, from the way that man's eyes had gone cold and black. Like a shark about to take a bite.

And if she lost to the big man, she might be more interested in taking a bite out of him afterwards and let Tavish slip out the side door and walk home.

He'd gotten a cab in. Usually walked back, mostly because the energy needed time to bleed off, and if he carried it back to his room, he'd be vibrating and have to go sit in a bar or restaurant for a time anyway.

Better to walk it out.

Sure enough, she pushed. Not everything in front of her, but most. More than she'd started with, so she'd come out behind.

Tavish folded when she did that, mostly because there was one card left and Gorbovich wasn't good enough to bottom-deal, so anything he'd set up drifted to the left.

Instead, Tavish sat back and watched. Zenkova was trapped, and had to keep playing. Kretov had her leash and jerked it a little with a raise. Mound of chips in the center of the table got pretty big.

Pocket change to most of the folks around the table, but Tavish could see where she was like him, once you got past the shell. Broke and hungry.

And about to lose what might have been one hell of a nice pot.

And down she went. Tavish didn't nod externally, but he'd set her up pretty solid. Then let Kretov have the killing blow, as it were.

He cashed in his chips when they were through. Pocketed a decent return on a night's investment, and tipped his hat to everyone when he recovered it, jacket, and gun from the butler.

Kretov had a ghost of a wink as he saw Tavish out the front door. The others were taking longer to organize. And would need to call staff and have the fly out skycars for pickup.

Tavish was done with these folks for now. Nothing new tonight except a new player in Zenkova, and he'd have lunch with Kretov in a week or two and get the gossip on the woman.

Kretov knew everybody in this town, which made him such a useful contact. Most of the things Tavish learned weren't valuable, except when aggregated into something larger.

Tavish's job was simply writing reports and sending them on. Others would interpret.

And act.

He got paid to play cards. And watch people.

Morning was crisp. Sun was threatening to turn the eastern sky a lighter line of color, but wasn't there yet. By the time he walked home, false dawn would be showing. Then he'd sleep for a few hours, get some lunch, and write reports this afternoon, while things were still fresh.

Out the front door. Down the long walk past the landing field that would be filling up soon. Out to the front gate and through, unto the roadway.

He had his hands in his pockets as he walked. Chill air. Still breezy.

Sound of skycars coming up from the city. Couple of them.

And a strange sound he couldn't place. Dull, quiet whomp, instead of the high-pitched whine of turbines. Getting closer, but he couldn't place it against the dark sky, except that it was downhill from him.

Coming closer.

Didn't sound good.

Then the sound got loud, and a hawk swooped out of the night.

Tavish had his pistol in one hand, pointed down, as

something landed in front of him and started disgorging bodies. Road was dark. People in dark clothes. Hardly any lights on the whatever it was that had landed.

Tavish had slid up against the brick wall on his left. No cover there. And this felt like an ambush, so he needed to run.

"If you move, I will shoot you," a voice announced behind him.

Shit.

TWENTY-SEVEN

Serge was tired. Stiff. He'd been sitting longer than he'd expected, but unable to move.

Game had finally wound down. Players sorting themselves into discrete units. Gambler, following intelligence briefing, had exited the building on foot and was heading his direction.

Down the driveway. Past the open field.

Through the front gate.

Right on plan.

Serge was moving in darkness. Landing area was lit, but there were a lot of trees and bushes about, so he was a ghost, drifting like smoke.

No hue and cry, so he got to the gate he'd slipped in last night. Still closed.

Open it a crack and watch for the other ghost. Listen for quiet footfalls.

Man walked by. Not oblivious, but didn't see Serge's eyeball in the wee crack of the gate.

Serge let him get by, then slipped out and pulled the gate most of the way closed. No sound. Man might hear it.

He peeked out, and saw a back, backlit by the town's lights below them. Serge pulled his comm and clicked send.

Target in motion. Trailing. Engage at the intersection.

That was a safe spot for Lori to land. Big enough to clear. Ground vehicles would have lights on. Skycars would pass safely overhead.

Serge set out in the man's wake, moving silently in spite of the concrete sidewalk. It was like he'd done this before.

Other players had rides coming, but Serge ignored them. They were off-property at this point, so Vasyly Kretov shouldn't care. Or maybe the man would see it all as some grand adventure, on top of everything else that had happened.

Serge didn't care, either. Comm went into his pocket. Type Three came out.

Ghost.

Boyce suddenly unmasked and came out of the night. Target got skittish. As expected. Drew his pistol, but hadn't given thought to being boxed in.

Not yet.

Boyce grounded. Perry and the team bailed out.

Man moved to his side. Realized there was no cover. Started to turn.

"If you move, I will shoot you," Serge announced in a quiet voice, pitched to reach the man.

Type Three had a stun setting. Really freaking nasty hangover inducer mode. You had to train by getting shot. Being on the receiving end.

Yuck.

Target froze. Man appeared to be smart enough to understand that he'd lost track of his perimeter and let someone else sneak up on him. Gun arm froze, which was why he was still upright.

Pretty was strong enough to carry the man. The others would need to throw him over a shoulder and lumber or something.

"What's the call?" Arleth asked.

"Drop the gun, hands in the air, don't make me shoot you," Serge replied. "Got folks want to ask you some questions, then the plan is to turn you loose."

"You shitting me?"

"You have information we want."

Serge left it vague. Mostly because he was operating on rumors instead of a solid briefing. Deck Officer and Knight seemed to be the ones with all the pieces. Him, Stevens, Perry, and Toshiko only had fragments.

Pistol landed. Hands went up. Squire Perry led the others up close.

Then Perry shot him. Arleth went down like a sack of potatoes.

"He was behaving," Serge announced.

"I'll carry him," Perry laughed. "Easier this way in the close quarters of the helicopter."

Serge shook his head and claimed the man's pistol. Then got out of the way as Perry put word to deed and lifted the unconscious gambler.

They got to the helicopter and lifted off, low and fast.

Boyce had been on the ground for twenty-seven seconds.

TWENTY-EIGHT

Maddox studied the man when they deposited him into an empty cabin forward. Perry and the others had brought him in stunned unconscious. Maddox didn't know why, but the others didn't seem bothered, so he took a cue from that.

Tavish Arleth was put in a chair and cuffed to it by both wrists. Legs could move, but he wasn't standing up. Toshiko wasn't here, mostly because she'd never met the gambler and he should have no reason to know her on sight.

Plus, that let her be a surprise later.

"How long will he be out?" he asked Nordin as she gave him a quick inspection.

"Maybe another twenty minutes, depending," she said. "Perry hit him with a Type Three at close range. Called it crowd control."

Maddox turned to the tall man. Noted the indulgent smile.

"Where's Serge Broom?" he asked.

"Arleth had papers on him," Perry replied. "Dropped Serge off to go into his room and grab anything that looked interesting, then catch a cab back to the ship. I expect him in about ten minutes."

Maddox considered it, then turned to the Doc.

"Leave him out for now," he decided. "We'll let him come around on his own. Maybe Serge will find something that tells us what we need to know."

"I'd have heard from Broom if he found the amulet," Perry interjected. "Assuming it moved on."

Maddox nodded.

"You watch him," he ordered Perry. "I'll catch Broom when he arrives and he can brief me if he found anything. Then we'll come down here and chat."

"Broom promised that we only wanted to talk to the man," Perry offered. "That we might just let him go later."

"Only if he tells me what I want to know," Maddox replied coolly. "If he gives me trouble, I might keep him locked up and haul him to Vhogga Base and ask them to check for warrants. Pretty sure a man like this probably has some. If nothing else, I've ruined his travel plans for a month, so it's in his interest to talk. Or we have deeper problems to address."

Maddox nodded to both of them and headed aft. Serge would board via the bridge tower access. Then they'd find out what he'd found.

TWENTY-NINE

Maddox was in the map room, sipping coffee and listening. It had been a long night, but he'd managed a nap, leaving Narayana to monitor things. It was going to be a long day, too, but he'd prepared.

"Sir, I think you need to see this," Serge Broom announced from the door, then stepped in and placed a book on the table before stepping back and coming to rest, hands crossed behind him.

Maddox picked it up and studied it. Eighteen centimeters by about twenty-five. Four thick. Normal looking. Printed paper, bound in leather or something with a similar feel. Red originally, faded down to something closer to salmon today.

He opened it to a random page, but discovered that the center had been cut out, providing a hollow spot a little larger than his palm. That held a smaller book. Maddox extracted it, looked up, and got a nod from Broom.

The smaller book wasn't written in any language he recognized, though the letters were all standard.

"Hidden in plain sight in his room?" Maddox asked.

"Aye, sir," Broom replied. "Couple of others, but normal. Clothing. Knickknacks. That sort of thing. Then this. Not sure what it is."

Maddox nodded. He was, but only because he'd been there at Albany, when *Marrakesh* had nearly gotten destroyed by a Leviathan in a nebula.

Because a spy aboard had been all set to broadcast a signal that would lead *Wronlori* to find them.

No way in hell he could have taken that monster in a fair fight, but Captain Boru had made sure it wasn't fair.

"Excellent work, Broom," Maddox said. "Grab the Deck Officer and send him my way, please?"

"Aye, sir," and he was gone.

Narayana didn't take long to appear.

"Sit," Maddox said, still thumbing through the smaller book.

"What's that?" Narayana asked.

"Pretty sure it's a code book," Maddox replied. "If you memorize certain things, you can encode them and only somebody who knows the pattern can undo it. Well, I suppose a Nav computer might have enough horsepower to brute force it, but nothing the average person is going to manage."

"Arleth is a spy?" Narayana asked nervously.

He didn't know the truth about who else Maddox worked for beyond Survey Corps, but he was a sharp fellow. Able to add two and two together and get an accurate guess about the sorts of things *Marrakesh* had done.

And for whom.

"That's my guess on first approximation," Maddox replied. "Sure as hell changes things about how we talk to him."

"Any idea who he might be working for?" Narayana pressed.

"Could be anybody, but this feels like something bigger than just pirates," Maddox said. "At least to me. Given the location, it could be any of the three closest powers: *Wronlori*, *A'Zedi*, or even *Traisa*."

"*Traisa*?"

"The *Enlightened Tyranny* isn't all that close," Maddox conceded. "But they are almost directly rimward from here, and there's a lot of open space, especially between us and *Wronlori*. Plus, they're generally neutral in the current war, while us and *Copez* are dealing with more *Wronlori* shenanigans."

"We still interrogating him?"

Maddox looked closer and realized that his Deck Officer was a little queasy. It was one thing to decide to randomly kidnap a criminal. Something else again when a mask might suddenly slide off and reveal a bigger issue.

"We are," Maddox said. "At the same time, I need to compose and encode a much bigger message to send home. And can't do that until I know more. He might be one of ours, in which case an apology will be appropriate. Same time, he might be our enemy, and we haul him home and make him disappear from history. They can decide what to do with him."

"What about Toshiko?"

Everyone called her by her first name these days, including both of them.

"I think she'll understand," Maddox said. "And I'll have to decide how much to tell her later. After I know."

Maddox rose.

"I want you to come with me as a witness, Narayana," Maddox ordered. "Things just got a little weirder than we expected."

THIRTY

Narayana followed Maddox forward. Empty cabin occasionally used as storage, but they had a place on the ground here that they could put things when they needed them. Toshiko was staying in the medbay for another week or two, depending on if you asked her or Nordin for a timeline.

He studied the gambler as they entered. Man was muzzy with stun wearing off.

Maddox closed the hatch and it was just the three of them and Perry. Even Nordin had been shuffled off outside, after one last check that the man was mostly recovered.

Stuns were usually safe. Sometimes folks had a cardiac reaction and needed immediate help. Usually an age thing. Or a secondary neuropathy.

Gambler looked as healthy as a horse.

Narayana watched Maddox pull out a tablet, set it on the cabin's desk, and turn it on.

"We are recording audio and video," Knight Nevin announced in that formal voice you usually heard as part of a court martial.

Gonna be one of those nights. Days. Something. Things hadn't settled since Jaffa's World, as far as Narayana was concerned.

"The man shackled to the chair is tentatively identified as Tavish Arleth, a gambler of some reputation, and not a known citizen of *A'Zedi*," Maddox continued. "You are awake, Arleth. The medic confirmed it for me."

Eyes opened. Pretended to be confused, but there was a hardness inside that probably wouldn't be obvious on tape later.

"Who are you?" Arleth demanded.

"*A'Zedi* Knight Maddox Nevin," he replied. "Commanding officer of the *A'Zedi* Patrol Corvette *Kalyn Blackford*. We are currently still in harbor at Hithadhel Port on Astarte III. That could change."

Narayana noted how hard Maddox's voice had gotten. Matched the gambler's. He figured that his job was merely to provide a second command officer witness, so Narayana slid to one side and leaned against the bulkhead next to Perry. He'd let the big man handle any issues that came up. Steve was tough enough. Mean enough.

And Arleth was still chained down.

"What do you want?" Arleth asked.

Wasn't a demand. Fellow understood that he wasn't holding any good cards at the moment. And Maddox still sounded polite. Just not friendly.

"I had one of my people go through your belongings in your flat," Maddox replied. "Found something quite interesting there."

"What?"

That sounded a little sharper. Angry, but there was fear under it. Narayana had gotten good at reading tones for secondary emotional signatures, after he and his crew had broken their next two commanders after Kumas Das.

Malicious compliance could be an utter bitch. You still needed to know when you had pushed exactly far enough.

"A book," Maddox offered negligently. "Came with a surprise inside."

Narayana noted that Maddox didn't say what. Perry wouldn't know. Arleth might not be sure of anything at this point, still recovering from an electronic hangover. He still had a flinch.

Bad time to be interrogated. Hard to control yourself. Even for a professional gambler.

Narayana was pretty sure that wasn't accidental on Maddox's part. Man was meaner and sneaker than he let on. And it came with a switch he could turn off, which made it all the more useful.

Arleth didn't reply.

Maddox nodded.

"I've seen something like that before," he continued. "On my previous ship, we had an encounter a few years ago. Something similar was involved when my captain got it all sorted. Tells me things about you, Arleth. Bad things. I'm not law enforcement around here, being outside *A'Zedi* space, but this isn't about legality, is it?"

Arleth flinched again, though he was getting better control of it as he woke up and settled. Still, he was giving himself away.

"Better, nobody can prove *habeus corpus* right now," Maddox said. "We have you in our control, but don't have to produce you for a local magistrate, because I cleared all this with those folks before we did anything."

He paused. Arleth added a bit of a shiver now.

"I can do anything I want with you," Maddox threatened politely. "Anything at all. And I might. Or I might not. Didn't set out to dig up your past and only accidentally revealed it this far. I was after something entirely else when I stumbled into your life. Tell me what I want to know, and I can stumble back out again. Maybe."

That was just the frosting, as far as Narayana was concerned. Maddox Nevin knew how to play hardball. That much was obvious. And was willing.

Certainly for the best that Narayana had warned this crew to get their shit back together and act like professional sailors. Maddox would have told command to break the crew up, blackball them all, and end a lot of careers unnecessarily.

Had they made it necessary.

"What do you want?" Arleth finally asked, after confirming that his hands had no range of motion.

"This is the best part," Maddox smiled cruelly. "I don't want information about who you're spying for. At least not yet. Pretty sure I can crack your codes and read that myself."

Ouch. Just, ouch. Kick the man when he's not looking.

"What I'm tracking is a red pearl necklace, with an iridium setting and a blue stone," Maddox said. "Original owners tracked it as far as you and hired me to recover it."

Narayana suppressed his snort. Only partly a lie. Maddox had decided that he owed Toshiko for her trouble, and was paying her back thusly.

Arleth was confused as hell, that much was clear. Probably expecting to be unmasked, though Narayana wasn't sure who they would find.

He'd read somewhere that spies like this were experts at living double and triple lives. Feeding people believable levels of bullshit to escape any situation, either to kill someone bothering them or make a clean break and vanish.

You couldn't trust them very far. But if they were chained down and given options, things might be acceptable for a time.

It would be highly embarrassing if he did turn out to be an *A'Zedi* spy, and unwilling to reveal himself.

"Necklace?" Arleth managed, even sounding a little normal.

"You won it in a poker game six months ago," Maddox replied. "Off a pirate captain. It vanished at some point and we're tracking it. Who'd you give it to?"

Arleth got cagey at that. Emotionally flat and bland. Nothing external as he processed.

Problem was, Narayana was pretty sure Maddox had gotten what he needed to identify the man's lies. He almost did, and Maddox was playing harder and meaner.

"What's in it for me?" Arleth asked.

"Once I have it in my possession, I don't need to bother you anymore," Maddox replied. "You tell me a planet at that point and I'll put you down on it and wave as you walk down my gangplank. Until then, I'm keeping you as a prisoner of war. And might just have to haul you to an *A'Zedi* base and turn you over so they can figure out who you are and who you work for if that takes too long. Obviously, your cover is somewhat blown at this moment, at least with my crew. At the same time, I could tell the Sabine Star and her people what I know. Maybe turn you over to them if you piss me off, since they have legal jurisdiction right now. Would that put a smile on your face? Pretty sure it would for me."

Okay, rude. Viciously rude, because that woman had a reputation for deadliness. But only if you crossed her.

Spy, operating in her city? Not an outcome most people probably looked forward to.

Maddox turned to Perry.

"I'm done for now," he announced. "Tough guy here will need time to process all this. Leave him free in this cabin, with a guard on the hatch outside. Entertainment unit turned on, but locked down hard. Feed him on a regular schedule. Let me know when he has something interesting to say. Otherwise, let him ferment and fulminate."

Maddox turned the recorder off and collected it. Nodded Narayana to follow him.

They ended up in the map room.

"What was that?" Narayana asked tentatively.

"A performance for a performance artist," Maddox nodded with a subtle smile, turning to fix himself some more coffee.

Narayana had had enough coffee to possibly float this ship at this point. He'd need sleep, so he planned to only drink water for the rest of the day.

"How long until he cracks?" Narayana asked.

"Might never," Maddox shrugged. "If he is a spy for *Wronlori* or *Traisa*—or even *A'Zedi*—he might stay in that role in spite of anything I could do to him. Not going to put much effort into it."

He sat. Narayana sat. Maddox keyed the intercom line.

"Expert Sailor Kellogg to the Map Room," he called, the sound echoing of walls. "Expert Sailor Kellogg, report to the Map Room."

Didn't take her long. Sweaty, so probably she'd been below on the treadmill, grinding out the kilometers like she did.

"Sir?" she asked, dabbing her face and neck with a towel.

Narayana nearly swallowed his tongue when Maddox handed her the code book.

"Make a complete copy of this," he ordered. "Use any scanner necessary, assuming things that might not be visible to the naked eye. Then translate it."

"What language, sir?" she asked.

"I have no idea."

Narayana watched her look up from the book in surprise, then crack it open and study it.

"Use the nav computer if you have to," Maddox ordered. "Might be a simple code, in which case I'd like to read the contents."

Blinks. Surprise. Maddox was treating the young woman like she'd already been commissioned as a Squire, when he didn't think she'd gone that far in her own head to consider it.

Still, she snapped to.

"Aye, sir," she said. "I'll let you know."

"Thank you, Kellogg," Maddox replied. "Dismissed."

"Now what?" Narayana asked when they were alone.

"I'm already playing hardball," Maddox replied. "Our friend gets to decide how far down that path he wants to go before he cracks."

"And if he doesn't?"

"Then Fleet Operations gets him," Maddox smiled. "And they probably turn him over to Intelligence Operations and they handle things. Not my problem at that point, other than we might get an extra gold star or three from some important people, if he turns out to be our enemy."

Narayana wondered who Maddox actually worked for. The man had connections that didn't make sense for a simply Knight taking a lateral to Survey Corps.

Right now, he was just glad they were on the same side.

PART 4
SECRETS

THIRTY-ONE

Stenny Kellogg held the book in her hand and wondered what the hell she was supposed to do next. Flipping it open, a jumble of random characters, possibly organized into words, but maybe just chaos.

But the Knight had ordered her to do something. She headed aft with it in hand.

Squire Morgan was in duty when she got there. They were Mutt and Jeff, with Morgan as short and muscular as Stenny was tall and lean.

"Whachagot?" the woman asked as Stenny got close.

"Need to check out a diagnostic probe," Stenny said.

"For?"

Squire Morgan was a hands-on woman, but also an officer.

"Knight wants me to scan this book, then decipher it," Stenny said, holding it up where Morgan took it and flipped it open.

At least she didn't have any better ideas than Stenny did, listening to the woman grumble.

"What is it?" Morgan asked.

"A mystery," Stenny replied. "My job to solve."

A nod. The squat woman moved to a bench and pulled out a drawer. A probe got extracted and handed over.

"Lemme know if you need something more advanced than this," she said.

"Honestly, I don't have any idea," Stenny replied. "If you think of something that might help, I'd love to hear it. Planning to scan everything visual into a system and see if I can find a way to translate it into something meaningful. Knight thought that there might be things only visible under certain scanners, so if you think an X-ray machine would work, I'm game."

Morgan opened the book again. Studied it closer while Stenny turned on the probe and confirmed that it was working.

"Why don't you settle in Kjell's office for a bit," Morgan offered. "I want to try a few things here."

Stenny didn't argue. It was a quiet spot with the Engineer off duty, so she settled and flipped through things first. Mostly checking.

Book was about half-full, which suggested something more like a diary than anything, since it was hand written numbers and letters in seemingly random blocks. Still, better safe than sorry. She started with the otherwise blank cover, a brown canvas that was glued on. Scanned it with every setting the device had, and offloaded the results to a new folder in the nav computer, because Nevin had said that was going to probably be useful.

Inside cover. First page of text. Second.

Took the better part of two hours to just go through every page, including the blank ones. Her mind danced with ideas of invisible ink, but nothing showed up on the scans. At least so far.

"Kellogg," Morgan barked from the main bay, so she rose and stepped out.

"There," the woman said pointing, so Stenny put the book down and stepped back as a bright light came on.

Almost blinding. Machine next to Morgan hummed louder to itself for several seconds.

"What is that?" Stenny asked when it stopped.

"We use it to look through metal plates into generators and engines, when we can't open them because they're running or highly radioactive," Morgan replied. "Machine is smart enough to peel off layers as it goes, scanning one depth at a time. Lets us reconstruct something in three dimensions and see cracks or casting flaws."

Stenny was a pilot. She knew stars and geometry. Mechanical engineering was a whole new thing she'd never really gone into. But the screen lit up and started showing designs.

"Back up one," Stenny snapped as the image flickered.

Morgan paused the readout, then ended up going back two.

"Oh, shit," Stenny muttered.

"Yup, tend to agree with you there," Morgan replied.

Stenny started typing, and navigating folder trees.

"Put everything here," she said. "Then wipe this machine's memory and anywhere that it backs up. Information involved needs to be you, me, Deck Officer, and Knight, until someone says otherwise."

She blushed as she realized that she was giving a Squire orders. E5 enlisted sailor telling an O1 officer what to do. But Morgan merely nodded and typed.

"You'll brief Nevin?" Morgan asked.

"That's my next step," Stenny replied.

Because shit had just gotten out of hand.

THIRTY-TWO

Maddox figured that he could get his body back on schedule next week. The last three days had seemingly run together in ways that were hard to tell apart. Coffee had been helpful for a while, then it started making him groggier.

Nordin had given him something that promised to clear his system out, which had the unfortunate effect right now of letting him hear color. Or something.

Or maybe Kellogg was just vibrating at the wrong pitch. Woman was hyper, but couldn't decide what emotion she wanted to land on today.

"Sit," he ordered. "Breathe."

He waited, drinking water that still tasted like battery acid.

Sleep. Soon. Not yet. Kellogg had found something big.

"Okay, talk," he said after she had calmed some.

Wasn't vibrating as bad, if nothing else.

She pulled up a tablet and typed. Maddox checked the clock, somehow unsurprised that it wasn't yet noon local.

He'd been going like hell overnight and then some.

"I have everything scanned with a diagnostic probe, sir,"

she began. "Squire Morgan put the book into one of her devices and did a thing kind of like an X-ray scan, so it would show interiors that we might have missed otherwise."

"What did you find?" he asked.

She turned the tablet around and handed it to him.

"This is inside the cover, sir," she said. "I'd have to take the book physically apart to actually touch it, but someone printed it with metallic thread, though I couldn't feel it and it didn't show up on my portable unit's scan."

Maddox pressed his lips together and nodded.

This changed a whole bunch of equations. And none, when he got right down to it. Tavish Arleth was a spy. He'd known that. Book practically screamed it.

And if the portable diagnostic probe missed it, then he wasn't an amateur about it, either. Professional.

And working for the *Traisan* Interior Ministry from the symbol. Not exactly the equivalent of *A'Zedi* Intelligence, but close enough.

"Who knows what you've found?" he asked Kellogg.

"You, me, and Morgan, sir," she replied. "I basically ordered her to keep it to the three of us and the Deck Officer. Everything is locked down under a password in the computer for now. Wasn't sure where to go next. Have the book contents scanned, but haven't started trying to crack anything."

Maddox nodded. She might not find it. Nyssa would have had it at her fingertips, but the right people had decided to hand that woman an atomic bomb when it came to cracking codes.

"You keep working on it, but at a lesser priority," Maddox decided. "I'll send a message home, but they're two or three days minimum getting back to us, and might order us to drop it and let him go."

"Sir?"

"We're not at war with *Traisa*, Kellogg," he reminded her. "They are neutral, and generally behaving. We're outside our jurisdiction. And kidnapped the man instead of arresting him. Locals will probably be most interested in what we know, but do not let them find out anything as yet. Questions?"

"Keep trying though, sir?" she asked.

"If you think you can read it, yes," he said. "Do not damage the book. Or tell anyone."

"I'm on it."

She bounced up and out of the map room.

Maddox reviewed the tablet again.

And started composing a message to Madame Gelashvili.

He had no doubts she would be reading it personally, when this tidbit exploded in her lap.

THIRTY-THREE

Toshiko had largely settled in on the ship. And taken a few trips into town, dressed in civilian gear more appropriate to the local culture than anything she had previously owned. Or preferred. Pants less baggy. Extra jacket as the weather was chillier on this planet.

Squire Perry had at least given her back her walking stick, so she felt comfortable if there was trouble in town. Not that she expected it, as the town was more urbane than anything on Jaffa's World, but that wasn't a high bar to clear.

Toshiko was still an outsider. *Amaechi* by birth. *Copez* by citizenship. Far from her home in the distant east. Facing legendary *Wronlori*, not too many light-years distant had she kept going.

Recommendations had led her to Bistro Himilco for dinner. She could finally eat food that wasn't bland and easy to digest, and wanted something more interesting. *A'Zedi* food, from what she's smelled, was a little dull and boring, but she didn't tell them that.

Inside the main door of the mall, she found the woman managing. Or at least commanding the forward flank.

"Mistress," the woman brightened when Toshiko got close. "Just one for dinner?"

"That is correct," Toshiko replied, following the woman.

She ended up seated at the bar. She supposed she could call it a bar. A half-meter or so wide, with a low wall that separated her from the kitchen itself, with the cooks moving around close enough that she could have reached out with her stick and touched one without stretching.

They moved with the seriousness of samurai as they cooked. Little jocularity, but she supposed that they were on stage here and had a reputation to maintain.

Or something.

The waiter got her settled, but one of the cooks took her order directly when she was ready. And began to work with the focus of a tea master serving the Court.

A man emerged from what she supposed would be a back office. Serious face. Brown hair kept short. Mid-forties. Knowing eyes that locked on her and narrowed.

No challenge, so Toshiko matched his stare, daring him.

To what?

She wasn't sure. This culture was strange. Different definitions of personal space. Or color usage. Everyone on the crew of *Doctor Kay* recommended she eat here, though. So she had arrived.

Toshiko felt a little out of place, then realized that most of the people she'd seen on this planet had darker skin and lighter hair. *A'Zedi* folks tended to be much darker brown than *Wronlori* or *Copez*, while her utterly black hair was darker than almost all of them.

The man approaching looked more classically *Wronlori*.

Pale skin not as white as hers. Green eyes. Maybe hazel, as he was approaching directly, having circled around the counter at the far end.

Toshiko placed the stick in her mind, but left it leaning against the counter for now as she turned her head. It was immediately at need, but he did not present a threat.

Still, one was always prepared, if violence suddenly arose.

The man stopped a respectful distance away and bowed his head.

"Mistress," he said. "New in town?"

"I am," Toshiko replied. "You come highly recommended."

"By the crew of *Kalyn Blackford*?" he asked.

Toshiko supposed that she should have been surprised, but folks had told her that this was a fairly small town, for all its size. Insular in many ways. Rumors would flow quickly.

And the crew had an obvious affection for the restaurant.

"Indeed," she nodded.

"Scott Hysmith," he introduced himself. "The owner. Can I get you anything special?"

She noted the way both cooks perked up, glanced over, nodded, and went right back to their tasks.

She'd done kata with less focus while being formally judged.

"This is my first trip out, sir," Toshiko replied.

"After you were injured, yes," he noted, so obviously the rumor mill had gotten here ahead of her. Again, she was not entirely surprised.

Sailors loved to gossip, and most of them knew hardly anything at all, save the quest itself. And even then, Toshiko didn't think that Nevin had told many people many details.

He gestured to the next stool over. It was mid-afternoon, and there were few customers at the moment.

"May I?"

Toshiko nodded, wondering who this man worked for. What rumors would he be seeking to clarify or expand? Or mislead?

Still, Nevin's crew respected the man.

He sat and one of the cooks delivered a mug of what smelled like tea.

"Will you be staying long in town?" he asked after sipping.

She did the same, mostly to consider her answer.

"I seek a thing," she said simply.

He nodded without comment, so someone had told him enough. How many people knew of her quest? Probably the power players on this colony, as Nevin had mentioned working with the woman who owned it. And hinted that they should meet at some point.

"Does its recovery involve an immediate voyage home?" he asked carefully.

"Probably," Toshiko replied. "I have been years at sea to find it."

"Honor must be served," he nodded back, surprising her.

But the two cooks nodded as well, overhearing the conversation in the quiet restaurant by being less than three meters away from her.

It was not a culture she was prepared for. Almost like being back on Metra, when she had been unconsciously expecting another pirate world, perhaps.

"Do you know where it might have gone?" she asked simply, offering no hints to see what he knew.

Or what lies he might offer.

"I remember the memory of it passing," he mused. "Five, six months ago. But it vanished as quickly as it arrived, a rock disappearing into the waters instead of skipping across."

Poetical. And in line with what Adrian and others had suggested.

Arleth did not have it. Hadn't kept it long. Whoever had it now was keeping things exceptionally quiet, too.

"People are looking, but it must be kept quiet," she replied.

Hysmith nodded sagely.

"If it was here, someone has locked it in a trunk and buried the trunk," he said. "I suspect that it left Astarte III instead, but couldn't begin to guess where it might have gone. Or with whom. Still, I will make a few discreet inquiries, and let Nevin or his people know if I find anything."

Interestingly, he rose and bowed, exactly as the cook finished plating her meal and delivering it before her.

A tightly run ship. Good to know. Adrian and others had all liked the bistro. Toshiko found herself respecting it, which was much harder to achieve.

And perhaps they could help her.

THIRTY-FOUR

Maddox had recovered for the most part. Slept a normal night. Narayana was getting calmer, but still a little twitchy.

Then the call came.

He was in his quarters. Mid-day. Relaxing with paperwork, because there was always paperwork to do. Waters was on the bridge.

"Sir, caller on landline for you," Waters said when Maddox answered the beep.

Landline. The ship had landed and planned to be here for long enough to hook up to local power and water systems. That included comm lines instead of radio, suggesting someone wanted a private conversation.

"Nevin," he said, opening the line.

"It's Asya," the Sabine Star replied with a hint of humor to her voice. "I came across an interesting tidbit that I wanted to share. Are you available for dinner tonight?"

"I am," Maddox told her.

Commanding officer was never off duty, but technically

not supposed to stand watch shifts, either, leaving that to the Deck Officer. Captain Boru, however, had trained him better than that.

"Scott Hysmith is going to deliver food just before sunset to my private quarters," she said. "Dress is casual. You'll be out late. All that acceptable?"

"It is, mistress," he smiled. "I shall see you then."

And the line went dead.

Obviously, something good. And an excuse to have something that might qualify as a date. Or at least a chance to sit with a peer and talk. In addition to being a beautiful woman—and rich—she was also something of an intellectual underneath it all.

Once she trusted you enough to let you see some of those deeper layers.

Maddox didn't suppose that most of the folks involved in shipping around here absorbed obscure literary fiction for pleasure. He'd had to expand his reading list, just to try to keep up with her.

He spent the afternoon sorting things out and prepping Narayana to handle whatever, but nobody suggested any alerts beyond good discipline, so he got escorted into town by Bachchan and deposited on Asya's doorstep, as it were.

She opened the door and presented a cheek for a kiss, then escorted him inwards.

It always amazed him, but her personal quarters had more square footage than his ship. Simply enormous, seemingly going on forever through wallless rooms more suggested by art and furniture than any cleaner demarcation.

They ended up in the kitchen, him seated at the long bar watching her check things in the oven and mix them drinks.

Maddox sat quietly and appreciated things, supposing that

a woman like her didn't get to be off duty very often, either. It was one of the things that made whatever they had work, because they could leave responsibility at the door for a time, knowing that they had sharp people capable of handling most things.

And he'd gotten to know Stefana Davidovich, a kind of Executive Vice President who managed the bordello below and could intelligently answer questions about most of the rest of Asya's domain.

She handed him a highball glass with ice and something caramelly, while hers was a mauve that wasn't far from the color of his shirt.

Maddox let her set the pace. As always. Woman could probably buy her own Patrol Corvette if the mood struck her. Or six.

Food got pulled from the oven and set for them to eat side by side at the bar, serving themselves from various dishes and bowls. Excellent, as always, particularly since Hysmith was involved.

"Has your prisoner told you anything meaningful?" she asked finally.

"The expected complaints and threats," Maddox replied. "My suggestion that we had cleared it all ahead of time with you did much to shut him down. At this point, he's merely being stubborn."

"I've checked, and he didn't open any sort of security box at any of the banks," she nodded. "Nor done anything exotic with men like Vasyly Kretov, who might be considered something of a patron to your prisoner."

"It was only a thin chance that he might have done something like that," Maddox shrugged.

"I did get lucky, though," she continued, eyes glittering now.

"Oh?"

"Phil Freund, at the paper, had been planning a newspaper article on local high-stakes gambling," she said. "I got the impression from him that it was mostly a puff piece intended to open up certain tourist avenues. Draw in some of the bigger players, as it were. Someone—not me—threatened him if he put it out, so he has sat on it for now."

"Not entirely surprising," Maddox nodded. "From what we've learned, Arleth won the necklace in a poker game where at least one of the players was a pirate captain. Possibly several. I don't suppose folks like that would be excited to suddenly have to compete on a bigger stage, though I'm surprised that he didn't come to you for protection."

"Me?" she asked coyly.

"You, who owns this city," he smiled. "And this colony. And whatever else strikes your fancy. Would Astarte III be better served if you had more folks like that coming here? Turn it into more of a resort and less of a smuggling haven?"

"I would, yes," she acknowledged smiling slyly. "Others would be less pleased. It comes back to most of them preferring to be big fish in a small pond, instead of vice versa. More money and development perhaps turns Astarte III into a giant stage, instead of letting it be a seedy backwater."

"If I'm successful, hopefully there will be less piracy around here," he said carefully. "Sure, folks will still arrive with cargo perhaps under-documented, but that's smuggling. The fencing of pirate goods, everyone could do without, I think."

"Don't mention that too loudly," she replied. "While I tend to agree, others are a bit too deep into their personal proclivities. You'd need to move slowly and carefully."

"Always," he said. "Never push too far or too fast. Let things develop, while guiding them in a certain direction."

Her smile spoke volumes.

"However," she said, taking a breath. "Freund. He may have a partial list of folks who were in the room when the necklace changed hands."

"Oh?" Maddox perked right up.

Had one of them stolen it later? Bought it off of Arleth? Otherwise fenced it?

And she could have sent it over, even via courier, so Maddox appreciated that she'd set them up on a date of sorts. An evening when they could enjoy themselves, leaving responsibility at the door.

"Are there any surprises worth chasing madly after?" Maddox asked her.

"There might be," she said, with a bit of evasion he couldn't place.

At least one of the players had been a pirate captain. Possibly several. And a few locals willing to play high-stakes games with such folks.

Dangerous ground, but Maddox was willing to stack his crew up against most. And he could always ask Fleet Operations for help.

A ghost touching his neck had him shiver unconsciously, but she saw it.

"What?" Asya demanded quietly.

"Had a thought," he offered, calculating how much he could tell the woman without getting either of them in trouble.

"Go on."

"While we were out on our most recent patrol, the one that took us to Jaffa's World among others, the *A'Zedi* fleet apparently hit a pirate base not all that far from here," he said.

That much, everybody knew, because it had been the talk of the town all week. Only twenty-five light-years away. Practically neighbors.

Still, he had an alibi, having literally been parked on Jaffa's World that day.

"And crushed it," she said.

He couldn't tell if she was pleased with the outcome or piqued. And now was not the time to ask.

"So they say," he said. "I'll have to return to home base to get all those details, most likely. Would the person or people we'd want to talk to have been there? In custody or dead right now?"

Because he honestly didn't know. There were certain details that would not be transmitted, since any code could be cracked eventually.

And he hadn't needed to know until this moment. It had been his job to set up the line of Science Stations that had tracked those pirates, once he knew where and how to look for them.

Fleet had come in at that point with a big, fucking hammer.

"That is always a possibility," she shrugged. "If nothing else, folks will be a while rebuilding over there, so they might not appear here for a time."

"So I'd have to go to them, if we found the person we wanted," he concluded that thought.

Then shrugged.

He didn't mention that Toshiko's pirates appeared to be a third group operating in the near vicinity, *Copez*-ward from Astarte III. And coreward some. Northwest of here on local maps.

Lots of open space over there. *Unaffiliated* worlds, sure,

but some that didn't communicate with outsiders. Maybe they just wanted to be left alone, he knew. Religious, cultural, or political movements like the folks who had once been the *Amaechi Concordancy*, though they stayed strictly inside *Copez*'s borders.

And he didn't ask Asya if she knew. Wasn't his place. Was one of those spots where they might be on opposite sides, more or less, with him serving law and order and her making money on chaos.

Still, fewer pirates and Astarte III might have to turn themselves into a resort town to make money. Different kinds of corruption, but the sorts that folks brought on themselves.

Pirates never asked permission.

They finished dinner with small talk. Had decaf coffee laced with cream and whiskey. Settled in a different part of the suite, a talking salon. They'd put plates and dishes away, and someone would come by in the morning to clean. If he was still here, they'd have the bedroom door closed.

"Excluding all of your peers," he began as they sat. "Would it be to your benefit if piracy got pushed farther away? I understand that some folks like Misho Pavlov make most of their money under the table, but he's going to get crossways with *A'Zedi* or *Wronlori* at some point and be made an example of. Not by me, but by someone. Or he'll get caught with a hand in a cookie jar, selling stolen goods that can be traced to him. If I wanted to clean up Astarte III, would you like that or find it objectionable?"

"That depends on what you mean by clean up, Maddox," she said, eyes bright with unspoken questions. "I'd benefit from legitimate trade. About half the others would, as well. The others might react poorly."

He nodded at that. About what he'd expected.

And now he had Freund's list of people in the room, against which he could compare notes and rumors.

And maybe, just maybe, another ally in Asya Orlova as he went about his task.

THIRTY-FIVE

Stenny stopped just outside the map room and drew a heavy breath. Focused everything inward. Her twin brother liked to tease her about being wound a little too tight, most of the time.

Today, he wouldn't be wrong.

Calmed, somewhat, she moved to the hatch and rapped the panel. Knight Nevin looked up and swear-to-god she thought he could see completely through her.

"Sit," he ordered, pointing to the other seat.

She did, understanding that most commanders would have her standing rigidly at attention while they spoke.

Most commanders were assholes, too.

"Find something?" he asked, studying her like she was transparent.

She was even too wound to blush at the thought.

"Might have cracked his code, sir," she offered in a voice filled with awe, fear, and finality.

"Lovely," he nodded. "What was the key?"

And just like that, he'd assumed she was right, accepted it

from an enlisted sailor, and jumped forward to what she'd learned.

Again, most commanders were assholes.

"Diary, sir," she said.

"How so?" he asked, intrigued.

"Man dated each entry, though it didn't stick out with punctuation or anything," Stenny replied. "Saw a pattern where chunks stayed the same, so I guessed that it might be a date. That helped me unravel everything else. Got the system walking through my scans, translating them and saving it all to a side-by-side translation document so I can go back and compare the outcome. Couple of places his grammar gets weird, so I've been studying *Traisan* culture to try to make sense of things."

"Gold star, Kellogg," he smiled, warming her. "Two, as a matter of fact. Maybe more, if you managed to take his entire life apart without us needing him to tell us whatever lies he thought we wanted to hear. What do you know about the necklace?"

"I don't think he knew what it was, sir," she told him. "I went to the entry about the game, once I knew how to read his date field, and came forward from there, figuring that was most important for now."

"And you are correct, sailor," he nodded to her. "Intelligence will want the rest, along with your notes, but I expect that they will also hand it off to a separate team to recreate everything you've done to confirm it."

Stenny wanted to ask what he meant by that. Something in his eyes held her back.

Maybe because he looked like a man who had worked with the spooks before? There were rumors, but nobody knew anything. Or those who did weren't talking.

Deck Officer seemed on the fence. Everybody else was guessing.

Maybe they'd been guessing right? Maybe that Radio Officer on *Marrakesh* was more than she'd seemed? Hard to tell from what the Knight had said, but still...

Food for thought.

"Do we know what happened to the necklace?" Nevin asked.

"This is where it gets weird, sir," she replied, sucking down a hard breath and locking the mad energy and vibrations down. "I think he gave it to a girlfriend. Or something. A female of some importance, who subsequently vanished with it. He was pissed at first, but the way I read it, he kind of shrugged and went on with his life, which seemed odd to me."

"If he was a spy, would she have compromised his cover?" the Knight asked.

Stenny had to stop and think about that. She didn't have a lot of experience with relationships, though her twin brother Benjy had been happily married to his high school sweetheart for six years now.

Could you keep something like that a secret? Or would it be too much work?

Could you even trust someone you met while living that kind of lie? And he was deeply inside a lie. Stenny had read enough of his life to understand that the man everyone else knew as Tavish Arleth was nothing like the guy keeping notes on people, places, and things.

"Maybe, sir?" she finally offered, uncertain.

And she really was the wrong person to ask, because she didn't do misdirection. You got what you got with her, and were happy with it, or you could move on.

Or she would move on. Had, a few times. Maybe about like this guy and the girl that had gotten the necklace from him.

Or was she another spy? Gun moll? Prostitute working her way from relationship to relationship, looking for something?

Stenny understood the *something* part. What was she looking for?

No clue. Maybe she'd dig deeper into this spy's life and see if there was something there for her to learn.

"But you know who she is?" Nevin asked, jarring Stenny back into the present tense.

"Got her name, yes," she nodded. "Octavia Haught. Described as a tall, busty, strawberry blonde that's natural."

She was blushing as she said that, having had to reread those parts to confirm the description.

The Knight merely nodded and ignored her discomfort. Probably for the best.

"Pull out those descriptions and rewrite them," he ordered her.

"Sir?"

"We're going to turn Stevens and others lose," he smiled. "I suspect that Arleth disappearing so completely from Hithadhel will have caused her to vanish herself, if she's still here. If not, she's still got several months head start on us anyway."

"Would she recognize Toshiko on the street?" Stenny asked.

"You tell me, sailor," he replied. "I want you to focus on the book translation. I'll clear it with Dr. Abbas and Squire Rackham, so you won't be standing bridge watches until you're done. Excellent work, Kellogg. Keep it up."

Stenny took the dismissal and fled, blushing, flushing, and excited at having solved at least part of the mystery.

Now, she had to solve the rest.

THIRTY-SIX

Narayana read the report, based on Kellogg's translations, Stevens's black marketeering, and a few other tidbits of uncertain provenance he didn't ask about. It all added up to something, but he was probably the wrong person to guess.

Narayana had always tried to color inside the lines. Even before all the problems that had originally gotten him grounded. Unlike Maddox, who seemed to have a much better understanding of how far outside he could get without drawing trouble down on his head.

Octavia Haught. Physical description of the woman practically screamed *Enlightened Tyranny of Traisa*, being tall and blonde. And Maddox had mentioned that Arleth was a *Traisan* spy. Was she also *Traisan*? From home? Some sort of secondary spy or partner that had split off to pursue other projects?

Too much unknown. And he still thought that there was a third pirate group out there, beyond one known and one destroyed.

Narayana looked up and caught Maddox looking back

from his side of the map table that had turned into the central command post for this ship.

"Science stations," Narayana offered.

"Oh?" Maddox asked.

"We've put down three rows of them," Narayana continued. "One found and isolated our friends for Fleet. Second and third as legs from Jaffa's World were going to track that other group we only have hints of so far. Is there a way to put down a third spoke from Jaffa, running directly coreward?"

"Parallax on folks west of there?" Maddox replied, seeing it immediately.

"Toshiko had tracked them that far," Narayana said. "Or the folks we're looking for live over there. Is there a way to track that elusive pirate base somehow?"

"Sure, but I can't imagine that we could take a whole base by ourselves," Maddox replied. "Nor do I want to, if we're only after one woman."

"And she's likely to vanish if and when rumor gets out that Arleth got captured by someone," Narayana said. "How do we run ahead of that news?"

He liked the way Maddox's eyes suddenly focused on a point about a thousand light-years over Narayana's shoulder.

Silence that stretched.

"Smugglers and pirates," he murmured. "Yes. WATERS!"

"Sir?"

Roland appeared a moment later, having been working in the radio room at the forward end of the bridge.

"How far could you track someone in Ghost-space, if we wanted to see them but not be seen in turn?" Maddox asked.

"Do I know where they are starting?" Roland asked.

"Here," Maddox pointed down. "We move off and park

quietly somewhere, then listen and watch someone moving by at high speed, following in their wake."

"Fifteen light-years, maybe," Roland shrugged. "Depends on a lot of things. Might be easier to plant another sensor buoy closer here and have it tight-send a signal to a point where we could camp, sir."

Narayana nodded. Sound move. Might need to not tell Orlova about it, though, as the woman might get a little tetchy at an *A'Zedi* patrol monitoring her port that closely. Even for a short period of time.

"Narayana, what's your estimate that a smuggler might be able to see us?" Maddox asked.

He considered it. Civilian gear. Maintained adequately, but not with the sorts of military focus of a standard line warship, to say nothing of a patrol cutter like *Doctor Kay*.

"I'd be surprised if they could focus at five light-years," he offered. "And even then, they'd have to be looking. Probably four if they were on general passive mode."

"Excellent," Maddox said. "Waters, you work with Forslund and Morgan to identify or build the device you think you'll need. Get it ready and then let me know. We'll spread some rumors around here, then take off and plant it, pausing out in the dark like an eel down in the rocks while we wait."

"Immediately, sir," and Roland vanished aft.

Narayana waited.

"I presume you have a plan?" he asked.

Then Maddox told him, and Narayana laughed.

THIRTY-SEVEN

Maddox got admitted to Asya's office, not all that far from the bordello at the heart of the Sabine Star.

"Your smile promises trouble," she said as he entered and sat across her desk from her.

"Had an idea," Maddox replied. "Hoping to enlist your help. Mostly rumor-mongering, as much as anything, but I think this rumor will flush the folks we want out into the open."

"You going to pounce on them?" she asked.

Doctor Kay had made her name in the vicinity by destroying that one pirate ship a few months ago. And perhaps that base that got smashed would be added to his bill at some point.

"Actually, no," he said. "Hoping to get them to run, instead, so I can track them to their base."

"You assume a different base than the one your cohorts just smashed?" she pressed.

"I do," he said. "If my target was there, I'll have to send notes home and see if anyone saw her, but the folks she was associated with weren't them, as near as I can tell, so I'm hoping she went elsewhere."

"She?"

Was that a hint of jealousy? Maddox kept his surprise under wraps.

"Arleth gave the necklace to a woman after he came into possession of it," Maddox replied, keeping his tone purely professional. "We have her name and description, but nobody has seen her on this planet for at least several months, so we presume she went elsewhere."

"And the rumor-mongering?" Asya asked.

"I'd like someone on this planet to put up a wanted poster, for lack of a better term," he said. "Tell the underworld that we're specifically gunning for her, but only after I've left in a hurry, like we've already found a lead."

"Because someone who knows will immediately haul ass after you to warn her," Asya nodded, seeing it. "What happens if she's with other pirates??"

"Then I track them to a set of coordinates," Maddox replied. "And look to see how tough they are. *Doctor Kay* can take a single cutter by herself, but not a squadron. Nor can we chase down a mob if they scatter. I'm coming to you because I think this is a group of pirates outside your immediate circle of acquaintances, as it were. Folks from a much more distance sector, where their loss doesn't impact negatively on your cash flows if they got disrupted."

"Most commanders wouldn't be so careful about civilian economies," she pointed out blandly, though her eyes were glittering.

"Captain Boru taught me a lot of lessons about honey and vinegar, mistress," Maddox replied. "I like forward homeporting out of Astarte III. But that means that you have a patrol corvette operating in your vicinity. Yes, we scout worlds and update sailing records. Yes, that will facilitate trade, because those records get shared. And yes, I have a personal thing about destroying piracy. It is a deeply anti-social behavior that the galaxy can do without."

"But you honestly don't care about smuggling?" she asked cogently.

"Failure of society and laws as much as anything," he shrugged. "People want something and taxes are too high or it is cultural taboo. Something. That's socialization. Piracy hurts innocents, while people choosing to take various narcotic compounds have social issues that should have been addressed, so it's on the government failures."

"You are an interesting man, Maddox Nevin," she nodded. "One of these days, I would love to meet your Captain Boru and see what kind of demigod he might be, since you blame him for how you turned out."

Maddox blushed.

"He taught me how to be an officer, Asya," he replied. "A good one. A good person, too. Can I ask a favor of your government, to help me locate and potentially smash more pirates?"

"Going to turn Astarte III into a resort town?" she laughed.

"You'll make more money," he smiled. "And have more fun. And probably have to bring in more workers looking to get rich, so now might be the time to go nail down a couple dozen square kilometers with good beach and mountains close by, where you could build a proper resort and filter rich tourists for their cash. Might have to properly *Unaffiliate* yourself at some point as a neutral third party located in the middle. Maybe hire your own mercenary navy to protect the colony."

"Not sign up with *A'Zedi*?" She seemed surprised.

"I think we're the best culture sure, but I'm also biased," he replied. "And you're in the middle, so don't want to suddenly be on the front lines of a war you didn't start. Better if everyone had a safe place to land and gamble and drink and vacation. Even warships, if everyone behaves."

"You are making it sound promising," she grinned. "What's in it for you?"

"A nice place to work," he said soberly. "Interesting people to meet. Friendly port for my crew. Maybe a gold star with Corps Command, but nobody knows how they think."

Which was only partly a lie. Madame Gelashvili would love to have Astarte III turn into a dedicated, commercial freeport. She could insert any number of spies here. And Survey Corps could push deeper into the interior with a good example for other *Unaffiliated* worlds looking for more trade.

Drawing the galaxy back into a greater whole, after everything had come apart several centuries ago.

"And this woman?" she circled back.

Maddox reached into a pocket and pulled out a chip.

"This has everything," he said. "If you are willing to help, we'll take off on emergency lift as soon as I get back to the ship, then disappear."

"And I'll flush them for you to hunt?" she said, eyes scintillant. "I'll expect a full report later. And some sort of reward."

"I'm certain we can negotiate something, mistress," Maddox replied with a grin.

Hell, he'd even enjoy it, but pirate hunting came first.

THIRTY-EIGHT

Maddox was on the bridge, but the Deck Officer was in charge. As it was supposed to be done in the books that covered this sort of thing. Sippy cup of coffee in one hand. Other hand resting on a bar he could use to hold himself in place as they maneuvered.

"Radio Officer, you take charge," Yadav announced, nodding to Squire Roland Waters as that man stepped fully clear of his little room, with Specialist Aliz Voros sitting watch today.

"Pilot, what is our deflection from target coordinates?" Waters asked.

"Eight-tenths of one percent," Stenny Kellogg replied. Maddox had her flying today for a reason. "Slightly beyond and a shade above exact center, sir."

Waters paused and then shrugged, with a, "Good enough," thrown in.

He moved to the console and pushed a button.

"Flight deck, what is your status?" Waters asked.

"Your bird is ready to fly," Dr. Abbas replied immediately. "Programming updated warm from ship's systems."

A nod.

"Flight deck, deploy your probe," Waters said formally.

Maddox felt the motion in his feet. A hatch aft opening to reveal one of the Vertical Launch System silos, followed by a bump as a mechanical catapult pushed it out and up.

Missiles on *Marrakesh* had been the same way, except that they were launched horizontally with a lot more oomph. And they were programmed to immediately rotate on internal gyros, then ignite thrusters to push all that mass into motion, before splitting into smaller component parts designed to impact a larger conic volume and forcing defensive gunners to have to engage that many more targets.

Here, it simply boosted softly. In a few minutes, it would engage local thrusters and come to rest, relative to the closest set of stars, then engage a multidirectional sextant to lock itself to a particular facing and wait.

Anything departing from Astarte III would be passively scanned, with the signal boosted in the direction that *Doctor Kay* was headed next, forward and to one side of the rough expected corridor of flight.

Anyone heading into *A'Zedi* space would be noted. *Wronlori* ships might and might not be in the cone. *Traisa* would let them vanish almost immediately, but Maddox was playing a hunch that the big players weren't involved here.

Or at least had someone so deep-cover that they wouldn't reveal themselves for something as small as this.

No, he was after competent amateurs today, understanding himself to be in that category, but operating with help. And a damned good crew.

They waited on pins and needles for the better part of five minutes, then a timer went off on Kellogg's boards.

"Sirs?" she asked, catching all three of them over her shoulder.

Waters looked at Maddox, and he nodded to man.

"Ahead on rotary thrusters," Waters ordered. "Get us clear and stand by for Ghost-space."

Maddox nodded again. Waters was young, but sharp. Professional at Radio work, but he'd likely end up being promoted a significant distance. At least if he wanted it.

There was a war on, and bodies were the limiting factor, but not everyone wanted to make the navy a career.

Maddox couldn't imagine any other life.

"Ahead on rotaries," Kellogg replied, typing.

She'd gotten better about interpreting things and making it work, after Yadav had explained that the two previous commanders would have required that Waters turn over command to him or the Deck Officer, who would then have had to issue explicit numbers and times for everything, *then* docked Kellogg or whoever was flying for not doing it exactly right.

Here, they needed distance from the probe. Nothing more.

"Kellogg, when you get far enough away, transition and take us to our next rendezvous," Maddox said simply, letting her know that he trusted her to do it right. To do it professionally.

To get them there without a dipshit commander browbeating everyone at every step.

Before and after taking command of *Doctor Kay*, Maddox had quietly inquired around. He knew many officers who respected Knight Avguri Senoky. Still hadn't found *anybody* who liked the man.

And that said a lot in this navy.

Waters retreated to his radio room, but he tended to be a quiet, nerdy introvert, most of the time. Exactly what Maddox wanted for what was coming next. Roland's boss, Armiger Freya Vilchis, was the ship's Diplomat, but that meant that she was the people person of the team. Noisy, happy, flashy. The one pressing flesh and glad-handing. Useful, especially in Survey Corps.

Maddox needed technical details today.

"How soon will we know?" Narayana asked as they jumped to Ghost-space and everyone settled.

"I asked her to give us a six hour head start," Maddox replied. "We're on schedule to have parked and be listening when that happens. After that, I have no idea how long until someone blasts out of port. She did say that nobody was scheduled, but we took off without warning and others might do the same."

Narayana nodded, lips pursed.

"How likely are we go be able to catch her?" the man asked.

It was Maddox's turn to shrug.

"Command is letting us play a lot more loose than other ships," he said carefully. "Partly, that's our luck lately, finding and doing things. Here, we're simply extending that string of listening buoys, so nothing abnormal."

"And if we find a base weakly enough defended?" Narayana grinned.

"We do have a small security contingent," Maddox noted. "Our ability to get into serious trouble outweighs our ability to get back out, so we gotta be sneaky about it. Or find a way to call for all our cousins to come over to help."

He didn't need to tell the man about the sorts of folks who would be listening for the next report in from *Doctor Kay*.

Even the crew were starting to wrap their minds around the fact that they were more than merely surveyors. And had come back to those levels of excellence that Kumar Das had reported on a regular basis.

Narayana nodded, unconvinced.

"And your commanding officer isn't planning to lead the charge," Maddox added, seeing that wariness recede a bit.

That was what had gotten Das killed.

"Long as we're clear on that," the older man said soberly.

It was Maddox's turn to nod. Narayana Yadav had seen Das as a son, in many ways. The youngster he had trained, before the events that got Yadav disgraced and grounded. Only a war and a lot of pleading had managed to get Narayana Yadav back into space, and then only as Kumar Das's Deck Officer, the younger man having been promoted past him.

Just like everyone else would be, because Fleet would never promote Armiger Yadav again.

Dumbass move, but doing anything else would require that they admit they'd screwed up in the first place.

For now, they were all playing a hunch.

THIRTY-NINE

More paperwork, but in the map room, because Maddox figured that things would either break shortly, or not at all.

The probe would keep monitoring traffic in and out of Astarte III for about a month, but he didn't expect many surprises. And honestly planned to ignore anyone not headed roughly three hundred true on the map.

Wronlori ships went northeast. *A'Zedi* south through west. Northwest was where he expected trouble.

"Sir, I have a possible contact," Kellogg called, getting Maddox to his feet and through the hatch in two strides.

He looked over her shoulder at the screen Waters and Voros were tracking and relaying. One ping, moving pretty quickly on a vector about where he'd decided lay trouble.

Freighters were usually in pretty good shape if they could maintain Mark Four. And few could. This one was pushing up against it, but he figured that they must be planning a high-speed run if they held it for long.

Still, possible contact.

"Track them and start looking for destinations," he ordered. "Waters, assume a commercial freighter and give Kellogg a safe zone to stay outside of."

Almost instantly, a ring appeared on the map. Target was about eight light-years away, moving lateral in such a way that they wouldn't get closer than five and a half.

"Do you have enough to shadow them?" Maddox asked her.

"Sir?"

"If you moved right now, on a roughly parallel course, anyone seeing us on a scanner wouldn't assume we were following them, Kellogg," he said. "If anything, they might look to be tracking us. I want to stay ahead of them until they stop, then keep going and circle back around quietly."

"Oh, yes, sir," she said. "Stand by."

Her hands flew and suddenly the ship was in Ghost-space again, puttering along at the same rough Mark Four as their target. Hopefully, they would look like another medium freighter on a scan board, but this particular path didn't get close to any inhabited worlds he knew, *Unaffiliated* or not.

Like they might be leading him to a previously unknown pirate haven.

He returned to the map room to find Narayana already working in a book.

Sure, everything could be electronic, but there were times when pulling a binder and flipping to the right page added that extra *something* that a screen just didn't give you. He supposed that other commanders might turn this into an office or day room, but Kumas Das had wanted his maps, and both Kosere and Senoky hadn't felt confident enough to change it.

"Kellogg, what's their current vector?" Narayana called as Maddox sat.

He listened to her read off a string of numbers and letters, then watched Narayana flip pages back and forth until he landed on a page.

"Thirty-one light-years out," he called back. "Look for a main sequence yellow and a large red dwarf in a tight binary. Plotted, but I don't show any navigational updates in forty years."

"Roger that, sir," Kellogg answered.

Narayana sighed.

"Roughly eight hours, assuming a bit of maneuvering and terminal work?" the man asked.

"Sounds about right," Maddox replied. "We'll track them for an hour or so, then I'll go off duty and take a nap while you follow them in. When we get close, we can look around. Maybe drop a temporary probe. Something. Then we'll swap and you'll nap while we figure out what we can do."

"Will they be sharp about looking for us?" Narayana asked.

"Initially," Maddox replied. "That's why I want Kellogg leading instead of trailing. If they get there and don't see us, they might relax, thinking we've gone the wrong way."

"After the wrong rumors," Narayana nodded. "Gotcha. Sneaky."

"Might have done this before," Maddox offered, without any other details.

Some of the things he'd done wouldn't be declassified while anyone who'd been aboard *Marrakesh* that day were still alive, to say nothing of still on duty somewhere.

Spies. But the fleet needed intelligence to do most things.

They shared a moment of camaraderie, then Maddox returned to the bridge and watched Kellogg work her magic. Subtle and off the target's forward port bow a considerable distance.

"Waters, make sure nobody is sneaking up on us or vice versa," he said, catching the man half in the radio room for a glance and a nod.

Not a lot to do at this point but watch and wait.

And hope he got lucky.

FORTY

Narayana had ordered Waters off duty and was standing both watches himself, with Kellogg and Voros doing their things and both understanding how delicate the situation was. Both women were the kind of crew members he'd want on duty at this moment, and Maddox and Roland would need to stay up late supervising once their Deck Officer got them to the destination.

Speaking of...

"Armory, Perry," Steve replied when Narayana pinged him.

"Deck Officer," Narayana replied. "Expect your full contingent to deploy to a planetary surface that we will arrive at in roughly nine hours. Whatever breaks, food, and sleep patterns they need. Have Boyce ready as well, since you might need to insert from a remote location."

"Found our gambler's moll?" Steve asked.

"Got a solid lead," Narayana replied. "Won't know what we have until later. Kellogg is tracking a suspicious ship in Ghost-space."

"Roger that," Steve said. "We'll be ready for the full team."

Narayana cut the line and paused to grab his binder from the table in the map room.

8989 Krittika.

Normal yellow star in a binary with a cool red dwarf. Several planets around that pairing, with larger giants in close and smaller rocks farther out. Combined heat from the two meant that habitable zone was wider than for most singles, and at a greater range.

No known colonies, at least as of forty-three years ago, when it was last visited by an *A'Zedi* ship, but that didn't mean anything. Not everyone checked in with the authorities before building.

Or let the rest of the galaxy know if they were open for business.

He checked, but Kellogg had everything in hand, even going so far as to drift her velocity up and down on a random pattern that looked like a badly-maintained autopilot while the crew slept.

Narayana approved heartily. She was coming into her own.

He moved to where Voros was working and watched her for a moment, catching a glance before she ignored him.

"If you were a pirate, how would you build your approaches?" he asked, startling her, but Aliz Voros was usually quiet.

Knitted in her spare time. And occasionally on duty when everything was quiet.

"Not like this, sir," she replied after a moment. "Fools might as well be erecting a sign on a highway. Place like this might be a roadside inn linking Jaffa's World eastward to *Wronlori* or Astarte III, then crossing *Unaffiliated* space back to *Copez*, where you didn't have to pay *A'Zedi* taxes or suffer cargo inspections on your caravan route."

Narayana nodded. *A'Zedi* was pretty good about maintaining and enforcing those borders. *Wronlori* generally attacked *A'Zedi* stations and fleets, and ignored *Unaffiliated* worlds, at least militarily. Diplomats flew every which way, but even the *United Technocracy of Wronlori* knew better than to piss off the independent worlds they traded with.

Bad way to ruin your economy, especially for *Wronlori*, who had a smaller population than *A'Zedi* or the others and relied more on automation to do things. You needed a lot of raw materials already semi-processed for your factories, and *A'Zedi* wasn't selling. *Traisa* was largely neutral, but farther away than places like Astarte III.

"Assuming our target, where would you expect to find the next world headed west?" he asked.

She seemed to have given this a lot of thought. Might as well take advantage of it.

After a moment, she brought up a second screen and fiddled, highlighting a ring of four stars.

"Probably inside this group, sir," she said, turning to make eye contact. "Scientific, wild-ass guess, though."

"Understood," he replied. "Mark a note for Waters and one of you remind me later to possibly drop another of our special stealth probes in that vicinity."

"We in the pirate hunting business these days, sir?" she asked.

"We might be," he temporized. "Fewer warships needed on patrol in this area means more fleet that can go punch *Wronlori* in the mouth and get them to behave."

She nodded. Typed.

Narayana stepped back and returned to his own station.

Maddox would need some of these ideas while they were fresh in his mind. Not that they would do anything today, but what were the limits before Survey Command finally jerked Nevin's chain back?

Who was his new commanding officer, anyway?

FORTY-ONE

Stenny had had caffeine. And a few munchies. Unless an officer ordered her off duty, she intended to sail them all the way in. And out again. Sagan Dituri was good, but not good enough.

Not for what they needed today.

She kept at her slide. Up to Mark Four point Three. Down to Three point Five. Rather random, in case anyone was listening on the right channels. Bad autopilot.

Former commanders would have thrown a fit. Or required approval for everything. Deck Officer merely smiled. Knight had noted things and nodded as well.

Felt good, exploring the limits of her professionalism. Even Das had been a little more wary about certain things, but Nevin had seen and done some crazy shit in his time, if even half the rumors were to be believed.

And the man was setting her up to maybe become an officer at some point. Her? Crazy.

But fun.

Stenny checked her clock. Her perimeter. Her flight cone.

Nothing had changed. Target had begun tightening his

flight path down on 8989 Krittika, like the Deck Officer had figured. Whether he was stopping there or making a turn, she wouldn't know until it happened, but she was all set to come around to starboard as soon as he dropped out of Ghost-space, even before telling whoever was in command at that moment.

They wanted this guy tracked, first and foremost. All the saluting and marching in squares was secondary. Kinda fun, if she could admit that.

A ping on her board nearly levitated her out of her seat.

"Radio, what's that?" she called.

Behind her, Knight Nevin was suddenly a presence. Not a bad one, either. Solid, like someone had just put up a building behind her. A castle or something. Safe. Tough. Stubborn.

"We're in outer band range of Target One, Kellogg," Aliz replied. "Got traffic coming in and out of your coordinates. Somebody just left and is headed roughly parallel to the nearest *A'Zedi* border."

"Parallel?" she mused aloud.

"They know where it is, and are remaining at a safe distance, Kellogg," Knight Nevin said quietly. "Assuming smugglers or something who don't want a customs inspection and fly quiet."

"Kinda hard to do that at these speeds, sir," she offered over her shoulder. "Been trying to look civilian, but there will be limits as we get closer."

"Understood, Kellogg," he said. "How soon until they arrive?"

"Twenty minutes or so?" she said, estimating by eyeball. "Figure they'll slow down as they get close, sliding off the speed to almost nothing before dropping out. Not everyone can program an autopilot to automatically hit a set of coordinates."

"You stay on top of them," he said.

Then she watched him lean in on the next station over and flip a switch.

"Engineering, Forslund," the man was on the line.

"In a bit, I need you to configure the Ghostdrives to go to stealth mode, Forslund," Nevin said. "We have a target, and want to sneak right up on him."

"Easier if we drop out first, sir," Kjell replied. "Take about ten minutes to make adjustments here."

"Kellogg will tell you when," he said, glancing over.

Stenny felt her eyes get big, then nodded at the man. He was counting on her to coordinate everything. To handle it. To act like she was already an officer.

More and more, it felt like something she could handle, too.

Now, she just needed to sneak up on some pirates.

FORTY-TWO

Maddox stood at the doorway to the map room and watched Kellogg and Voros work, hardly needing to speak, and then mostly to answer questions as they came up.

Probably exactly different from most of their experiences, but Captain Boru had expected his crews to handle things. If he'd dealt mostly with officers on a larger bridge, he still had high standards.

Maddox was merely extending that to Expert Sailors and Specialists in these two ladies. They could handle it.

"CONTACT!" Voros called. "Target has dropped out of Ghost-space."

"Coming about now," Kellogg answered. "Range five point eight light-years and steady. Engineering, I'll need about ten minutes to get you where I want to drop, then you'll do your magic before I begin my stalk."

Maddox nodding, unable to help the grin on his face. This might be the perfect spot to drop another of Abbas's special probes, but he was out. Might need to convince Command to send him out next time without a dedicated flight path, so he could drop little surprises along the way.

Like right here, not far off the path that some other ship had flown, headed due west outside *A'Zedi* borders instead of jogging inward to trade with *A'Zedi* merchants somewhere along the line.

He'd already added a couple of sets of coordinates to his personal log. He'd update Narayana after all this, and they could talk to Command when they circled back through Vhogga Base.

Today, he was in the survey business. At least one presumed so.

He watched Kellogg and Voros issue orders to more senior people. And handle things, because he'd set them up to succeed already.

"Stand by for Ghost-space," Kellogg announced on the general intercom. "Ahead Mark One and stealthy."

"Kellogg, how long until you start making mistakes from exhaustion?" he asked her.

Woman jolted, but Maddox didn't figure most officers would see it that way. She was excellent and he wanted her handling this. She'd still been on duty all day. And handling the hardest part.

She paused, obviously weighing her words, but he smiled to reassure her.

"An hour here to make sure, sir," she finally said. "Then a couple hours break for a nap would be enough to get me back on point."

"You sort it out with the Deck Officer and Dituri, then," he decided.

Her smile was a thing of joy to behold. Woman had never been allowed to be herself, obviously, but he didn't have her story. Merely what three previous commanders had to say about her, and he'd had to check the files to make sure all three were actually talking about the same Stenny Kellogg, from their various interpretations.

Maddox watched the system creeping inward. Mark One. One light-year per hour. Slow. Old, worn out freighter speeds, barely limping along.

Except that Forslund and his people had made adjustments to various systems to reduce their normal signature. Couldn't do it all the time, because efficiency went to hell, but it let them fly ultra-quiet.

That mattered today.

Narayana appeared. Scanned the log while Maddox watched Kellogg and Voros work.

"What happens if she immediately runs?" he asked quietly. "If some ship lifts off ten minutes after they arrive. Do we chase?"

Maddox grimaced. He'd had several hours to work out possibilities, and that was the utter worst case. Chase, or try to land and find her.

No good answers.

"Ask me again when they do," he finally replied.

Narayana nodded and moved to the map room. Maddox heard the coffee robot go to work, but he'd had enough for now.

Ship was quiet, in spite of the distance and stealthiness, but he understood that to be a way of thinking.

In fact...

He moved to a station and called up a command board, then lowered the lights twenty-five percent, and adjusted them down into a more yellow ambiance. More like firelight in a campground.

Voros looked up with a moment of panic, then saw what he was doing and cackled once quietly before shutting herself up.

"Sir?" Kellogg asked.

"Quiet and sneaky," he replied. "Body does what the mind tells it."

"Oh," she said, finally seeing it and smiling. "Aye, sir."

"Now," he announced. "Take us in."

PART 5
PIRATES

Fortunately, nobody had run. Maddox would take the little victories when he could, as *Doctor Kay* slid into the system and listened.

Between them, Voros and Kellogg had even nailed down the specific planet the target ship was visiting, from a distance. Everything they did now, finally outside of Ghost-space, would update all fleet's records on this area.

Including the fact that there was some sort of colony on the ground.

Again, small victories, that whoever was working here hadn't put a station in orbit. In fact, nothing but what looked and sounded like a weather satellite as they slid closer, everything passive and quiet.

Maddox and his Deck Officer had both swapped naps, meals, and downtime. Like a good command team should. Both were here, now, because things were about to get serious. Hopefully, not hectic.

"Radio, what's the local environment like?" he called.

"I'm reading ships on the ground, sir," Waters replied. "Mostly shut down but our bird is among them."

"Anyone watching the skies?"

"Not actively, sir," Waters said. "Nothing I can do about passive, but it doesn't look like anyone is paying attention."

Maddox turn to his Deck Officer.

"Quiet pirate base in the middle of nowhere?" he asked. "Don't do anything to bring attention on yourself?"

"And don't maintain any sort of formal, planetary government, either, I'm willing to bet."

"Not taking it," Maddox nodded. "Kellogg, can you get us around to the back side from our target's landing zone?"

"Easy enough, sir," she replied immediately.

"Good, handle it," he ordered. "Then be prepared to fly in-atmosphere at a low altitude to get us just beyond the horizon from them. Radio, I need topographical maps updated."

"Coming up, sir," Waters answered, but Maddox was watching Kellogg for a nod, after a deep breath.

She could handle it. Just needed the confidence to walk right up to that door and kick it open in her mind. And she was getting there.

"Oh, and update *Pretty* and his team," he added, catching her smile because Squire Perry was occasionally called that by most of the crew.

That man would be front and center shortly. Him and his team.

FORTY-FOUR

Steve had known not to roust everyone. Security and ground operations were always "hurry up and wait," sorts of things. Always took longer to come to fruition than folks expected.

Crew needed to be able to react instantly, but that had simply meant that he'd had everyone cleaning weapons and confirming them. Checking gear and repacking. Eating, sleeping, putting on game faces.

Somehow, he wasn't the least bit surprised when Toshiko walked up and smiled at him. On the taller side for a woman, but shorter than him. Everybody on this ship was shorter than him.

"I will be accompanying you," she announced, no doubt whatsoever in her voice.

"Clear it with Nevin," he fired right back, causing her mind to stutter for a moment.

Hard to do that to the woman. Hard focus, most of the time. Still, he caught her off-guard. Smiled to take the sting out of it, but if she intended to go with him, the Knight would approve first.

She nodded after a moment. Took her stick and walked right past him without another word.

Serge was close and spoke after Toshiko had left the chamber.

"You don't want her with us?" he asked.

"Wild card, Broom," Steve replied. "She'd be great as a distraction, but that's her out front scouting, like Stevens does for you in Hithadhel Port. Need Nevin approving it, because it's our asses out on the line if we end up launching a full frontal assault on a pirate base."

"I'll pack extra Molotov cocktails in that case," Porter spoke up from a corner.

Since he handled demolitions for the unit, not an idle threat.

"Do that," Steve replied, adding enough emphasis to make it an order. "Not going to be like Jaffa's World. Might end up having to shoot our way out of this one before we're done."

"Not the first time," Vanya noted. "Should I be carrying the Light Disruptor Cannon on this operation?"

Steve considered it. Big, bulky, heavy, and awkward. And damned useful when you needed to hit someone from a great distance. Or shoot down aircars.

"Yes," he said. "Everyone will be loaded for bear. If they don't start trouble, there won't be any. If they do, I expect you to stomp it into the mud and kick it a few times to be sure. Am I clear?"

Nods and assents.

Ground team ready to go.

Game faces looked back at him.

Ready for trouble.

FORTY-FIVE

Toshiko made her way up to the main deck and paused at the top of the ladder, not yet on Nevin's bridge but poised. She made a noise that got him to turn.

It required the man a moment to understand, then he nodded and she entered.

Toshiko was the outsider here. Nevin and his crew had bent over backwards to make her welcome, but she did not wear their uniform. Was not under their orders.

All of this activity they had undertaken was because Nevin felt it to be the most correct—most honorable—course of action to take, and both his superiors and his crew had agreed.

The taste of that in her mouth still surprised her regularly. *Copez* was an entirely different culture, and she began to wonder if *Amaechi* would be better suited to pack up all the ships permanently and move, save that they might have to disentomb all the ancients in the process.

And would the *Holy Imperium* allow them to leave peacefully?

They were allied with *A'Zedi*, but that was an outside war.

Inside, *Copez* still understood that *Amaechi* had been corralled. Not conquered.

It would be a delicate line to walk.

One she would undertake after she returned successful from her quest.

"Mistress?" Nevin asked as she came to rest in front of him.

"Squire Perry requires your approval for me to accompany his team into the field," she told him. "I request such a thing."

He paused and studied her. Not as a man admires a woman, but a warrior studying a stranger. Friend? Foe? Both? Neither?

"You would be required to follow his orders in the field," Nevin said carefully. Delicately, even.

"As is to be expected," Toshiko replied. "However, none of you could identify the amulet from a copy. Plus, I am an exotic unlike any ethnotype that one might encounter in such a place as we have journeyed to."

"I have only hope and intuition that we have identified the location we seek," he countered.

"And sound logic," she corrected him. "The plan is good. I do not wish to change it. Merely to supplement it with a layer of misdirection, because I find it highly unlikely that the woman in question would have a good description of me."

"She might have been warned of your tribe, Hajós," he noted.

Toshiko shrugged.

"Let her flee me," she said. "If that means that you chase her down with your ship, I can keep Perry and his team alive on a strange world until you return."

He wanted to challenge her on that point. It was there in his eyes, but he withheld. Nodded. Assented.

She watched him open a comm line.

"Armory. Perry."

"Toshiko Hajós will be joining you for ground operations, Squire," he told the tall man. "She understands that you'll be in command."

Toshiko nodded. Perry knew the team because he was their commanding officer, while she knew them as students of the open hand forms she had been slowly teaching them. None of the sailors were more than white belts in her arts at present, but all were veteran students of the dojo floor and would pick it up soon enough.

Perhaps she would need to return to test them at a later date, so she could award Shodan belts. After all, all the first black belt indicated was that a student was serious enough to have made significant progress. And willing to work forward from there.

Perhaps she would teach more of them a broader curriculum.

And scout a place where *Amaechi* might land, if they withdrew from *Copez*.

Toshiko bowed to the Knight and withdrew from his bridge.

She was prepared. Now, she needed to put herself in a place where she had a team to help her.

It was a novel concept.

FORTY-SIX

Steve watched the sky, but knew that Waters and others would warn them if anything suddenly took off. Still, old habits died hard.

They had landed on the planet. After flying low to get close to a town of some sort. Not too close, but close enough.

Lori Boyce had broken out that damned helicopter again and gotten it assembled. He'd have preferred *Packrat*, but there was no hiding that it was an *A'Zedi* cargo runner, whereas the whirlybird was unique, as far as he knew.

Like with the run on Arleth, team had stripped down and wore civilian clothing the Coxswain had made up for them. Even Vanya's cannon was strapped to the outside of the cargo box, mostly for space. Just enough gear to handle surprises and survive for a few days rough, but looking around, Broom and Bachchan could hunt wildlife and keep the rest of them alive if it came down to it.

And if they didn't have a posse on their asses. There was always that.

"How quietly could you fly this beast?" he asked Boyce.

"If the weather is calm, I can feather the blades pretty flat," she said. "Like this. We can get close and then get quiet."

"No hiding that we're here, but I'd like to not make a big splash," he told her.

Quick count of noses. Luck of the draw had sunset coming on. And them coming out of the east, so the darker part of the sky.

Him and Toshiko, more or less as officers. Serge Broom, Vanya Dowe, Porter Zavaleta, Sankar Bachchan, Trinity Diseth. Lori Boyce flying. Space to cram one tall woman in and lift, if they had her and could get out quietly.

Or not so quietly. Whatever. Pirate planet.

"Listen up," he called, drawing heads around. "This is a pirate world. That means that we are not enforcing the law here. Or even caring what it is. *Unaffiliated* places announce that shit, and have governments in place. This is a bar, a truck stop, and a chop shop, and likely not much more. Do not hesitate to unleash overwhelming force if you feel it necessary. Those are direct orders from your superior officer."

That last part meant that he'd be the only one facing a court martial if shit went sideways, but he was a big boy and could handle it. The others didn't need to worry about being second guessed later.

"Alright, folks," he said. "Mount up."

Time to go see a man about a horse.

FORTY-SEVEN

Toshiko had never ridden in an aircraft such as this. Loud, but a different kind of noise, it it rotated blades to generate lift instead of riding thrust.

She was up front with Lori Boyce while Perry and his team were in the cargo box aft. That way, if she got out, it might look like she was alone, allowing her to penetrate the city without drawing attention to herself.

Toshiko was exceptional at that sort of thing.

"Where do you want to land?" Lori asked.

The engines still made noise, but she had done something to make the rotor quieter. Possible to sneak quite close.

"There," Toshiko pointed. "On the northern edge of that landing field, away from the other ships but inside the berm."

"Coming up."

The woman piloted with precision, sliding in low and settling.

"Cut your engines like you will be here a while," Toshiko said, turning to open a door aft. "You wait here and watch for a time. I will enter town and start scouting."

"We've got your back," Perry replied.

Toshiko opened her side panel and stepped out. Evening. Warm, but it would fall to cold later, as they were on the verge of autumn at this latitude.

Still, she walked away from the bird with a firm step. A woman who knows what she is going and following a plan. Whatever it might be.

Town ahead, with a large berm wall around an enormous field that currently had eleven starships parked on it, ranging from one not much larger than the helicopter to two beasts twice the size of the cutter that had been her transport for the last month.

Toshiko walked up over the berm and descended, staring at the backs of buildings that all seemed to face away from her. Or towards one of the streets that ran haphazardly through the middle.

Cattle roads, if the world was old enough, but all of these buildings were new, so folks had built in the next available space, often using shipping containers cut and reshaped to purpose.

Not a lot of external lighting, even though there were two moons up, as neither provided much light.

Toshiko relied on stealth to move. It got her close to the center of town.

Not close enough.

Movement on her right as someone exploded out of an alley of pitch darkness between two buildings. Hand on her upper arm. Another sliding around to get a grip around her neck.

Mugger.

Not a particularly good one, either, but she could smell the alcohol on his breath as he exhaled.

Toshiko ignored him, save to mark the center of his rotation and join it in a dance.

Too many people tried to resist. To react to an opponent. The secret was to do kata and ignore him, save as he became part of it.

She turned into the rush. Slid under the grip because he had been expecting her to remain still. Her fist came up and smashed his grip away from her arm, with the pommel of her walking stick following to jab him under the ribs.

Painful place to be hit, male or female.

She stepped forward and turned, nearly behind him as he tried to understand what had just happened. Toshiko hooked his leg with her foot and pressed, letting his mass and momentum trip himself.

Not wanting to get dirty, she slid away as he went down, then smashed him hard with the blade still sheathed, pommel first into the hardest part of his skull.

Crunch.

She knelt, but he was unconscious and would remain so for a time.

Toshiko went ahead and emptied his pockets, keeping a small pistol of some sort and all of his money, with the rest scattered at her feet as she rose and walked away.

Not much different from Jaffa's World, then. A rough place, playing by rough rules.

Let them try.

FORTY-EIGHT

Maddox had a tablet monitoring orbital space, but nothing had changed in the last few hours.

That was good. His fear was having to deal with someone running, because he had a team on the ground and would have to decide if he picked them up first or left them to fend for themselves until he returned.

No, that wasn't it. He'd retrieve them, then outrun someone who thought they could get away. *Doctor Kay* was fast for a patrol corvette. No way a freighter of any size was getting away from him.

"Narayana, what's the status?" he called, watching as the man stepped into view from the bridge.

"All quiet," he replied. "Boyce just dropped Toshiko. Perry is waiting a few more minutes then slipping into town as a backup."

He would have liked Broom or Bachchan to handle that, but understood that Toshiko had far more experience at that sort of thing. And would be exotic, whereas his people would look like *A'Zedi* citizens.

"Let Boyce know that we might have a hot pickup mission for her, if someone lifts off," Maddox ordered.

Narayana paused, then nodded, while Maddox went back to waiting.

FORTY-NINE

Steve had the group break up and spread out. Boyce was staying put for now, armed and with all hatches locked in case there was trouble.

He got to the berm and counted noses.

"Serge, you and Trinity take the right flank," he ordered. "Sankar, you and Vanya on the left. Porter, you're with me until we find something to blow up."

"Lemme know which one first," Porter murmured, but that was Porter.

Pyromaniac who was pretty good at keeping leashed.

Steve walked high enough up the berm to look over with his extra height, then waved the others into motion. Up, across, down.

Dark town, with lights on a pair of squares ahead, brighter left than right. Just like Toshiko and Boyce had seen, he started after the right side first, assuming that his target wasn't necessarily going for the most noise, though he'd circle back if he had to.

Looking for one needle in a haystack the size of the galaxy. Or a fox, down in the swamps.

Best to use a hound for that sort of thing.

He paused, knelt in the shadow of a building as the other two teams stopped.

"Bridge, Waters."

"Do we know which ship it was that delivered our messenger?" Steve asked.

Pause.

"Negative, Perry," Roland replied. "Use your intuition?"

"Will do."

Yeah, he was afraid they'd say that. Never got close while it was flying. And everything on the field was a freighter of some sort.

He eliminated the two monsters because there was no way in hell they were keeping that sort of speed. And the littlest one could probably outrun *Doctor Kay* if they tried.

Eight in the middle.

"Boyce," Lori replied when he changed channels.

"Did you have a chance to scan everyone flying in?" he asked. "Looking for identifying marks."

"Uhm, gimme a second, Pretty," she said.

He waited.

"Got a portable IR handheld," Lori was there a moment later. "Third one on my left, with that weird dorsal fin, is hotter than everyone else. Like atmospheric friction cooling off. That would be my guess."

"Thank you," he said, then cut the line.

"Booby trap?" Porter asked hopefully.

"Maybe," Steve replied, waving folks back together. "Porter, you and Trinity rotate back and keep watch on that ship, in case someone exits or returns. They might be bringing our target to us. You have the description, so kidnap her and anyone else you have to, then call for backup or extraction, depending. Vanya, you stay with me while Serge and Sankar go into dumbass pirate mode."

Serge helpfully picked his nose and looked at it, gone all slack-jawed in the blink of an eye.

Steve waved them into motion, then set out to follow.

Best he could do to keep a cork in that bottle.

At least for now.

FIFTY

Toshiko followed sound and light. Let it guide her to a place just off of one of the squares, a side door into the quieter part of a saloon, where there was a large drinking room facing the open space.

Eleven freighters did not contain anything like this population, so she understood that this was a base where criminals could retire and relax, away from law enforcement.

And hungry onna-musha. She had the pistol taken from the drunk, plus all his cash, as she entered the smaller side of the establishment, noting the quality of clothing and sharpness of eyes turning to look at her as she made her way to the bar, fellows on both sides of her pulling back some to create a bubble of space that engulfed her.

Stranger, arrived at night in a place where folks would be surprised.

Story of her life over the last several years.

She possessed a blade, if things became untenable. And a wound in her belly that had finally healed enough to only twinge occasionally, reminding her of luck, both good and bad, and karma.

"Rum," she told the man behind the counter, putting *Wronlori* bills on the counter.

Big man, that bartender. Look of a former brawler, professional or amateur, who had gotten pummeled before getting out. Rough ears. Scarred hands.

He poured from a bottle into a glass that was clean enough to be sterilized by the concentration of the liquid inside. Pure ethanol, probably from a cooling system, with flavor and color added later.

A weak imitation of the real thing. Well, strong enough to strip paint, but rum by courtesy only.

She took a second sip and rotated in place, watching the room watch her. Heads nodded and went back to what they had been doing. Conversations came back up in volume. A classically trained pianist started a new song in a corner. Not a composer she knew, but expertly handled.

Two games of cards in motion, though neither for high stakes. Folks wandered into a bar and passing the time for entertainment value. As she had expected, having visited enough worlds like this to perhaps become an urban geographer on the topic.

Toshiko did a thing that made her emotional signature shrink. Let her vanish in place. Men on both sides ended up a half-step closer, but not close enough to touch. Her face was not inviting. And she had turned her back on the bartender, precluding conversation, but tracked him as he moved off to her left to pour for another customer.

Tracked the entire room, but did not see her prey. And Octavia Haught would have stood out in here from Arleth's description. Tall and bosomy. Curly hair in masses. Well-dressed.

The woman could have affected a disguise, but none of the women Toshiko could see were even close enough to warrant a second glance, being a roughly even mix of sailors of both genders on shore leave—perhaps officers from dress or at least successful merchants—and prostitutes wearing hardly anything and working perhaps the most honest trade this nameless world recognized.

Toshiko doubted that most of the sailors veered that close to professional honesty. The room had a feel to it. Too much like Jaffa's World, or a dozen other places she had transited in her quest.

Still, she waited for a time. Listened. Watched. Scowled sufficient to cow one man who looked upon her with a gaze of lust and expectation.

And she bore a blade.

Several minutes passed. She had begun think her instincts had led her astray, when a side door opened and her target emerged, following a rolypoly man in an overstressed girdle and excellent suit. They were in an obvious hurry.

Octavia Haught locked eyes with Toshiko across the room.

Nodded.

Started running.

FIFTY-ONE

Serge had point, with Sankar meandering along like a sidekick. Sankar was pretty good at this shit, but the man understood that Serge had been doing it a lot longer. And deeper into various roles.

Two men, both armed civilians with attitude problems. Semi-dark town, walking from one pool of light to the next with a stride suggesting you should be the one to get off the walkway instead.

Rough town.

Folks moving about, but a lot fewer than he'd been expecting for a place like this. Too early? Too late? Not a farming world, so no reason to go to bed early for cows.

At least he hadn't heard about anything like that during the flyover.

Most predators came out in darkness. Like him tonight.

Serge grinned at his own joke and turned into an alleyway, cutting across and certain that Pretty and Vanya were following with enough firepower to level this town.

And Porter was always ready to destroy shit.

Noise.

Serge tapped Sankar on the arm to stop and rotated his head like an owl turning on the targeting radar.

There.

Motion with it.

Someone hauling ass. Like, seriously.

Considering the where and when of his night, Serge nodded and started cutting across.

Not a lot of fools ran towards trouble.

Good thing he was one of them.

FIFTY-TWO

Steve had lost the two trouble-makers in front of him. Ducked sideways into an alley, but weren't there at the far end when he arrived.

Crap.

He nodded to Vanya and started jogging. Might blow their cover, but a woman running around with a Light Disruptor Cannon slung on her back wasn't exactly low-profile to begin with.

Not as heavily armed as both of them were over and above that.

Still, he wasn't enforcing any laws tonight beyond minding your own damned manners and leaving strangers alone. You wanted trouble, he could deliver.

End of the next alley, he paused. Mostly listening, because too much darkness around. Music from a couple of different bands or DJs. Hard to tell, because he hadn't spent any time in this town and anything was possible.

There.

Movement. Someone running. Single person. Head down. Hauling ass.

Steve paused to review the streets as he'd seen them from the top of the berm.

Running towards the port reservation.

Good thing he'd kept himself flexible.

"This is Perry," he said, causing Vanya's pocket to vibrate with a message. "Boyce and Porter check in."

He waited. They'd be digging comms out of pockets, listening quietly, then deciding how and when to respond.

"Boyce."

"Arm yourself and stand by to capture a runner," he ordered. "You have the north flank. Porter and Trinity are guarding the ship you identified earlier."

"Roger that," she replied. "Signing off."

"It's Porter. We got incoming?"

"Highly likely," Steve said. "Runner here. Movement your direction. Remember why we're on this rock."

"Standing by. You moving to flank?"

"From your south," Steve agreed. "Boyce has your north. I think the bobsy twins are herding someone your way."

"Setting everything to stun."

Steve didn't comment. Should have already been on stun. Hopefully, merely a figure of speech.

But it was Porter. You never knew.

He waved Vanya to keep up and turned right.

FIFTY-THREE

Toshiko felt the comm vibrate, but she was busy chasing after Haught, after getting caught up in the crowd in the bar. Folks possibly getting in her way just enough on purpose to slow her down and give her prey a head start.

And the woman only had to run faster scared than Toshiko could chase angry.

Fat man in the nice suit hadn't even tried to keep up with the woman, peeling off and going down a side street like all the devils in hell were coming for whatever sins he had tasted.

Toshiko ignored the man and kept her eyes on the woman. Tall. Taller than Toshiko. Longer legs, it seemed.

Not in as good a shape, but fear lent her strength to keep the distance unchanged.

Still, Toshiko could keep this up all night and a day if she had to. She had run-walked ultramarathons in her early training, and a month off hadn't cost her much in the way of endurance.

Haught wasn't getting away from her.

FIFTY-FOUR

Serge paralleled, two streets over. Streets? Something. Two rows of buildings with regular enough intersections that he could track his fox. Moving at a decent clip, but Serge was moving a lot faster.

Didn't like it, but had to cut across those two blocks before they got to the port. Maybe run whoever it was down short and take them in. Needed to keep them in sight.

He ran.

Cut across when he got there. Sankar was starting to lag. Serge would give him hell and make sure Pretty assigned the man significant amounts of treadmill time later, because Sankar had apparently been slacking.

Or worn the wrong boots for this sort of shit, which was a cardinal sin in this game.

Two blocks over, he turned and kept going, losing Sankar but holding a pistol in one hand.

Body just at the top of the berm and descending, vaguely backlit for a moment but Serge needed to run them down right now.

He hauled ass.

FIFTY-FIVE

Steve let his long legs carry him, eyes up and pistol centered forward with the safety off.

Stun on movement. Maybe stop, maybe not.

Berm.

Body going over berm.

Steve nearly shot Sankar in the butt, before he recognized the guy.

Centered his path and chased.

Up the berm.

Top.

Down the back.

Beam fire.

Steve sidestepped automatically without breaking stride, then zagged a step later.

Only the one shot.

His pocket vibrated.

He pulled the comm blind and thumbed it.

"Perry."

"One target down," Porter announced. "Stunned. Middle

aged male attempting to board our target ship. Wouldn't take no for an answer. Made him."

Steve nodded. Warning, then shoot.

You could do that with stun weapons.

He glanced and Vanya was keeping up.

Steve aimed at the freighter and followed Serge and Sankar in.

"Just the one?" he asked as he stopped.

"Just one," Porter replied.

"We only had the one," Serge added. "Caught him running like hell and gave chase. This was the ship that came in, so pretty sure that this was the guy who brought the warning from Astarte III. Kinda recognize him from town, but don't ask me his name. Ran with the money crowd, so Nevin might know him."

"Where's Toshiko?" Steve asked, looking at his small mob.

All six of them. One prisoner.

Not the wrong prisoner, but the wrong prisoner.

Then he heard another ship ignite its thrusters.

FIFTY-SIX

Toshiko cursed herself.

Haught could outrun her. At least far enough.

The woman entered the port reservation through an open gate well away from where Lori had parked the helicopter.

Toshiko had gained perhaps ten meters on her in half a kilometer, but only had a stranger's pistol and no way to tell if it had a stun setting. And it was too dark to look.

She ran in pursuit.

They crossed the port field in darkness and heavy breathing.

Toshiko heard a shot on her left. Too distant to be helpful. Possibly the fat man being taken. In her arrogance, she hadn't thought to call for assistance, and now it might be too late.

Haught reached one of the smaller craft, opening a panel and getting in. The hatch closed before Toshiko could draw and fire.

And she lacked the tools to do much more than watch. Certainly, she stopped running, because Haught could use her thrusters offensively if she had any skills as a pilot.

Toshiko moved into the shadow of one of the large freighters and vanished into darkness.

She had believed that she did not require assistance of any kind to complete her mission.

As the freighter over there began to lift, Toshiko discovered that she was happy to be wrong.

FIFTY-SEVEN

Steve heard engines and ran.

Vanya was close, already unlimbering the cannon for a shot. And probably good enough to hit something, going away in darkness.

Except what good would that do?

Little sucker lifted on a pillar of flame, but didn't get high. Vanya had the cannon in a standing pose, already centered and waiting for him to give the order.

Steve considered it. Seriously.

But they were here to retrieve stolen goods. Knight Nevin had made it clear that this planet was outside *A'Zedi* territory. Outside its reach.

Not their problem.

And they could always run the woman down again later. All she had right now was a bit of a head start.

Nothing more.

She wouldn't get away.

Then a star detached from the heavens and began to descend.

FIFTY-EIGHT

Maddox had directly assumed command.

Any mistakes this ship made would cost Narayana his career, in spite of everything the man had done right. In spite of being right, and being selected to take the fall for someone else's fuckup.

Maddox had to protect him. Especially as far outside the lines as they were coloring tonight.

"Kellogg, lift now," he called. "Stand by for pursuit."

She glanced up, nodded, and started typing.

Everything went from quiet to noisy. Hatches sealing. Sirens hooting. Thrusters igniting and starting to generate enough lift to carry a patrol cutter to orbit.

"Waters," he called over the noise. "Any updates?"

"Negative, sir."

Maddox nodded. Shared a look with Narayana that conveyed volumes.

Instinct. Maddox was willing to admit that he had nothing to go on, save for a ping in his gut telling him that endgame had already begun.

That he needed to move.

Now.

"Sir, course?" Kellogg asked.

Maddox listened to that voice in his head.

"Get me elevation and prepare to swoop on the port," he replied. "Warn Boyce that we're coming in hot overhead, so she doesn't freak out."

He leaned over to the comm.

"Gunnery. Veillon."

"Missiles are useless in atmosphere, Armiger," Maddox reminded her. "Unlock the turret and stand by to engage an aerial target."

He could heard her gulp. Particle cannons weren't much smarter in an atmosphere, but better than antimatter/matter thrusters. That would produce a mess, even on a pirate planet.

He wasn't here to enforce the law. He also wasn't here to destroy the place.

Any more than necessary.

"Weapons live, sir," she replied.

He cut the line and considered.

Everything he could think of covered. About to blow his cover and surprise, but it felt right.

"Radio, I have contact with the ground!" Waters yelled loud enough to turn him completely around. "Kellogg, one ship lifting from the port. Our target is aboard it and Toshiko says that it might be fast enough to get away from us."

"Kellogg, get me above her," Maddox said simply. "Now."

The ship lurched under his feet, but that was a pilot taking him literally. Engaging thrusters in lateral motion and riding the gyros around like a hawk on a thermal. Maddox grabbed a stanchion put there for exactly that reason and watched her screens from over her shoulder.

Narayana staggered forward like a man with a good drunk, but that was the deck moving under his feet.

Ship had been at red alert already. Everybody was ready.

Willing.

Able.

"Radio, target designated!" Waters called.

A red reticle appeared on Kellogg's screen, highlighting a ship in the process of lifting.

Small, sure as shit. Probably fast and agile.

Maybe even outrun an *A'Zedi* patrol cutter.

"Veillon, give me one shot across her bow," Maddox said into the intercom. "If you need to hit the ground with it, try not to damage anything important."

As in, fire now and worry about complaints and court martials later.

He watched a lightning bolt strike a spot outside the reservation. Hopefully a spot nobody lived.

"Waters, give me a wide channel."

"You're live broadcasting, sir."

"Attention enemy vessel," he ground out the words heavily. "This is the *A'Zedi* navy. Heave to and land, or we will shoot you down out of the sky and crash you. You have been given your only warning shot. The next one shatters your hull. Land *NOW*!"

He leaned back and slammed his mouth shut.

That ship either went for it, or discovered that he could chase her down and had gunners capable of hitting another ship in Ghost-space.

Hard to do, but Veillon had already done it once.

As had her commanding officer.

He watched. Waited.

Prepared to fire, because Toshiko had identified it as their target. The person or at least property that they had chased for a month.

Or years, in her case.

"I have red shift down," Waters called. "Repeat, target has cut thrust and is descending. Looks like they can make it inside the berm, or land just outside."

"Notify Perry and vector them down," Maddox called. "Kellogg, keep us hovering where we can fire if they try to lift again. Or anyone else does. Guns, stand by to engage any threat."

Brutal order, if he had to give it.

Wouldn't stop him.

Kellogg's hands were sure on the controls. Almost like they were on the ground, but the roar of thrusters through the hull was a dull pulse of anger that matched his soul right now.

"Message from both ground teams that they are converging on the target," Waters announced.

Maddox studied the plot of the starship reservation. The locals would be pissed and probably troublesome shortly, so he needed to handle all of this quickly.

"Kellogg, as soon as Perry takes possession of that freighter, get us on the ground," he ordered. "Have Boyce recover immediately after that. Waters, locate everyone on the ground and get them accounted for, so we can withdraw from this planet as soon as possible."

Maddox shut up at that point and let his crew work.

Time was tight, but they were professionals.

And he could always blast his way out of this situation if he had to later, fast enough to outrun anything heavy, tough enough to handle anything light.

It might come to that.

FIFTY-NINE

Steve got there first, leaving Vanya and Porter to handle the fat guy he'd shot and dragging Serge along. Toshiko was making good time, but Steve wanted to be in charge when this went down.

It might matter, if they were about to commit piracy. The *A'Zedi* navy had a lot more authority than one crazy samurai woman from *Copez*. Maybe not much, but enough tonight.

Ship was down and cooling. His boots were tough enough to handle the heat, so he crossed and banged on the hatch.

It opened and Steve got a look at Octavia Haught. Just exactly like her description. Tall, busty, gorgeous.

Pissed enough to chew nails, but he had an Adjustable Disruptor centered on her and a hard smile.

"We're here to take you into custody," he told her. "Nothing more."

"You're *A'Zedi*?" she snapped."

"Squire Steve Perry," he nodded. "*A'Zedi* Patrol Corvette *Kalyn Blackford*. She's overhead and was the one that fired on you. Do you surrender?"

Helped that he had Serge on one side and Toshiko on the other.

Also helped that she was currently wearing Luthien's Amulet. Platinum setting. Blood red pearls that stood out against her pale skin and low-cut bodice.

"Via, yes," she said. "What the hell is this all about?"

Toshiko stepped closer.

"I am Toshiko Hajós, onna-musha of the *Amaechi Concordancy* in *Copez*. The necklace you are wearing was stolen from my clan lord, and I have been tracking it."

"From *Copez*?"

Woman seemed surprised as hell, so Steve wondered how much Arleth had told her. Or how much he knew, because that one had kept his mouth shut.

Sure as shit was going to be surprised when she got added to the prisoner list, since he hadn't talked.

Nobody needed to tell him about the code book Stenny had cracked.

His smile might be a bit ugly, given how Haught flinched at him. Then Toshiko.

"Remove the necklace," Toshiko ordered.

Steve had a thought.

"How big is the interior of this vessel?" he asked, prodding both women into the hatch and to a mud room with a suit hanging on a rack.

He ignored them after that and stepped fully in.

Studio apartment. Cockpit at the front end. Bed at the rear. Bathroom on one side and closet on the other. Kitchen/salon/whatever in the middle.

Woman had decorated it. No masculine tendencies anywhere. He poked his nose in everywhere anyway and pulled a comm.

"Bridge, Waters."

"It's Perry. If you sent over a pilot who could handle this craft, we could depart immediately and rendezvous in orbit. Safer, I think."

"Stand by, Squire."

"Steve, I can fly this class," Toshiko said.

Somehow, he wasn't surprised. Probably easier to make a list of the things she couldn't do.

Shorter list, at least.

"Waters, belay that order. I can carry my team aboard this craft. Meet you topside."

"Perry, it's Nevin. We confirm the mission was successful?"

Steve turned to Toshiko, holding the amulet. The woman nodded.

Serge was in the hatch, waving people closer.

"Affirmative, Commander," Steve replied.

"We'll see you in orbit, then."

Steve smiled at Haught's confusion.

"We're just here to recover the necklace," he told her.

"What about me?" she replied, utterly lost.

"Knowing my boss, we'll be sending you on your way shortly. Possibly with a surprise. Dunno if its a good one."

He ignored all of her questions as Serge and Vanya got her searched and then tied her to a chair in the kitchen and settled around her. Boyce was already in motion, so they lifted off, crowded to the gills.

Wouldn't do for more than a day. Life support probably badly overloaded, but not his problem, and Haught could land immediately afterwards, because Steve knew that Nevin would kiss her on both cheeks and send her on her way, once Toshiko got a chance to confirm the amulet.

It was nice, being the good guys.

SIXTY

Maddox sat in the map room and tried not to smile too much as he watched Tavish Arleth and Octavia Haught scowl at each other. Perry was behind both of them, unseen. Smiling.

Both were seated nervously and not being a problem. At least so far. They'd rendezvoused in orbit, taken most of the crew of the smaller ship aboard, then turned and run like hell for a dark spot well away, with Boyce flying the small freighter instead of Toshiko.

That might matter later, if Haught tried to press charges for kidnapping and armed piracy.

They'd had two days, but Haught hadn't said anything meaningful.

Maddox had them in his map room because he wanted to see the looks on their faces when they realized what came next. Toshiko appeared at the hatch and slipped past Perry and Broom, coming to rest in the other chair where Narayana usually sat. He was nearby on the bridge, actually commanding.

And listening. And watching, because Maddox had heard the snorts as the man watched Toshiko enter.

She put an anvil case on the table. He had no idea why they were called that, but they were. Big box for a briefcase, more or less. Fifty centimeters long. Thirty-five tall. Twenty thick. Some sort of heavy-duty alloy Kimmel and Calder had come up with for this.

"What's the meaning of this?" Haught demanded.

Arleth had shut up early on and stopped talking about anything important once Maddox stopped asking questions.

Maddox ignored her and smiled at Toshiko as she opened the case, then spun it around.

"These are copies of the original," she announced, pointing to three perfect replicas of the amulet he could see peeking out from under Toshiko's shirt around her neck. "Madam Haught, you may pick one for yourself."

"WHAT?"

"My purpose was to recover the original," Toshiko told her in a hard voice. "I have done so. You acquired stolen goods in an honest mistake. The crew of this ship have assisted me in making perfect copies. You are free to accept one."

"Then what?" Haught snapped.

"Then I put you and Arleth on your ship," Maddox interrupted. "And back away before transitioning to Ghost-space and leaving. We are not pressing charges against either of you, but you both might want to exercise care before returning to Astarte III, since rumors suggest both of you are spies for *Enlightened Tyranny of Traisa*."

He rather liked that jolt of panic that bit both of them at the same time, like he'd flipped a switch and run a current though the floor.

Madam Gelashvili had gotten copies of the original book

and Kellogg's translations, and sent along a note that she didn't feel the need to have Maddox bring him in as a prisoner at this time.

After all, blowing his cover that badly pretty much rendered him useless, going forward.

Or maybe he could turn to full-time gambling and hope he could outrun news of his other employer.

"You're serious?" Arleth demanded.

Maddox nodded and smiled.

Haught took a moment, then tentatively reached out and claimed one of the necklaces like it might bite her. Nowhere near the value, but just as pretty.

She held it like it might be toxic.

"Perry, send them on their way," Maddox looked up at the tall man. "We're done with them."

The tall Squire dragged both out and aft, where they would be put in Haught's ship. Whether they got along or killed each other afterwards wasn't his problem.

"Kellogg, when you get the word from Perry, bring us around and lay in a course for Astarte III," he called.

"Aye, sir," she called back.

He smiled at the galaxy.

Toshiko looked at the remaining two and picked one out, putting it on the table in front of him before closing it up and rising.

She wanted to ask questions, but refrained. Instead, she bowed and withdrew.

They'd drop her at Hithadhel Port and she'd start the long journey home, though he understood that she planned to travel a good chunk of it inside *A'Zedi* territory instead of outside.

He'd sent Madam Gelashvili a note to that effect,

suggesting that she send someone to meet Toshiko Hajós and take that woman's measure.

Might be useful later on, to have a contact inside the former *Amaechi Concordancy*. Especially one that was about to return successful from an epic quest into the east.

Narayana appeared when the space got cleared out.

"Why did you have Camden make three copies, anyway?" he asked. "Never got that bit."

"One for Haught, to replace the thing we were taking from her," Maddox replied. "One as a spare for Toshiko, so she has something to distract the next thief that comes along."

"Yes," Narayana settled. "It's the third that eludes me."

"Asya," Maddox said. "She'd been helpful. Friendly. Stepped in and pointed us after the bad guys so that we could complete the mission. This is her reward. Hopefully, she likes it, though she did request a copy for herself. I really don't think she appreciated how good our Ms. Fixit was at this sort of thing."

"I don't think even Camden Morgan understood how good she was," Narayana laughed. "It's damned near a perfect copy."

"And there will be other copies eventually," Maddox said. "But only one original. Like the woman carrying it home where it belongs."

Narayana pursed his lips as it on the verge of asking. The silence stretched.

"We likely to ever see Toshiko again?" he finally asked.

Maddox shrugged.

"Anything is possible, my friend."

SIXTY-ONE

Maddox wouldn't admit it out loud, but he was getting more comfortable in the building that housed *A'Zedi* Intelligence Operations.

Big room hadn't changed. It hadn't changed. Empty space that could have held fifty on the empty wooden benches. Long counter separating three older civilians with scowls from Knight Nevin in *A'Zedi* purple. Day uniform, so no awards. Just rank and patch for *Blackford*.

The door behind the civilians opened exactly on time and Permanent First Secretary Mariami Gelashvili appeared. He watched her absorb the room, as if confirming that Maddox was alone on this side of the divider.

"Nevin, could you join me, please?" she asked the otherwise empty room.

He rose and made his way through the halfdoor, following her into the depths of *A'Zedi* Intelligence. Or something.

As always, numbers on doors. No names. Everything anonymous.

He understood why a lot better today than he had.

She led him to the office on the end, then pointed at the chair on this side.

He sat when she did. Waited with the sorts of infinite patience that Survey Corps instilled in you.

"I've read your reports, Maddox," she began after a long beat. "You danced eloquently around certain topics, but I'm not certain that most of the folks who read it would see that."

He tried not to blush. This woman was at least as smart as Asya. Probably just as dangerous. Permanent civilian head of intelligence around here, so most likely a retired field agent like Tavish Arleth had been, before the man utterly vanished.

Gelashvili watched him and nodded.

"Tell me more of your impressions of Toshiko Hajós," she ordered. "The parts you left out of your reports to Survey Command."

Maddox had been expecting this part. And kept the...more public parts...strictly professional, simply because he knew he'd be sitting here discussing them eventually.

"Samurai, ma'am," he began, then walked through his and his crew's impressions of the woman.

They'd left her on Astarte III, but Maddox had put in a good word and she and Asya had seemed to bond, to the point he wasn't worried about Toshiko getting home.

"From there, she walked down the gangplank and vanished into town," he concluded some ten minutes later. "We lifted off and returned to Horwin for refitting and a crew break, after maintaining a higher operational tempo than most of my sailors probably expected when they signed up originally for Survey Corps."

She was smiling at that. It was good.

"We've done some deeper research on the Amaechi Concordancy," she replied. "It backs up what you uncovered.

Conquered but not absorbed. Fiercely retaining their culture, one very much at odds with the Holy Imperium of Copez. We do not currently have active agents in place there, but I expect that the powers that be there might be more open to entertaining communications from A'Zedi, once this woman returns home with her story."

Maddox nodded and waited. Woman hadn't asked a question or invited a comment, and she was the ultimate boss as far as he was concerned. Even Survey Command listened to her suggestions.

"I've given thought to that space beyond Copez, Nevin," she said after a beat. "On all our maps, it is functionally marked 'Here There Be Dragons' for all anyone knows what lies there. You are certain that Amaechi vessels specifically never cross that border?"

"My impression was that they feared not being allowed to return if they did," Maddox agreed. "They live almost exclusively shipboard these days, only returning home to family tombs for holidays and special events, with a rotating cast of family members maintaining clan compounds, as well as elders who have withdrawn from the trading life. If I suggested that they were a pearl, hidden inside the oyster that is Copez, I think that describes them."

She smiled at that.

"While we are currently at war with Wronlori, Copez continues to be our ally, Maddox," she explained. At the same time, that could change without notice. The Holy Imperium has no love of the Technocracy, thus they ally with us. They have not forgotten dreams of imperial glory that would involve conquering the known galaxy. Given that A'Zedi is their closest neighbor, we watch them constantly."

Maddox wasn't surprised. Smart move, with Copez more or less behind A'Zedi, given the warfront in the east.

"I have spoken with Thaddeus," she continued, referring to Fleet Marshal (F3) Thaddeus Drayton, Chief of Staff, *A'Zedi* Survey Corps. THE Boss. "Given all your noise smashing pirates in the northeast recently, he agrees that shifting *Kalyn Blackford* to a different mission on a different frontier for a time might be wise. After all, we don't want your cover blown."

He grinned at that. They might be getting a bit of a rep with certain folks. Bad people, but word would get around. Useful if you wanted to drive piracy off entirely, but he and his crew had also laid out a couple of extra observation bouys, hiding them quietly on what folks had taken to calling game trails, just outside of A'Zedi space, where smugglers and miscreants might travel.

Useful to watch and learn. And maybe do something later, after folks had a chance to relax without an *A'Zedi* Patrol Corvette sniffing around.

"Where do you need us, ma'am?" Maddox asked her.

"You'll be getting sailing orders in a week or so," she replied. "They will take you to our southwest border, almost exactly opposite where you have been working. There, you will lay in supplies and take command of a small argosy that will include at least one cargo vessel, loaded to the gills with supplies for you. That force will sail to a set of coordinates that we believe are an inhabitable but uninhabited world, where you will stage forward. The cargo vessel will deposit everything, then return home for more, while you and *Doctor Kay* will run a long survey path that generally parallels the outer edges of *Copez*-claimed space, at a distance of some forty light-years."

"Edge of the map," Maddox replied.

"Indeed, Maddox," she agreed. "We'd like you to push it back some. Not that we expect anyone out there beyond fringe colonies and mining operations, but you were also there when *Marrakesh* went to Sabahattin, so you will at least be somewhat prepared."

"Anything in particular we're looking for, over and above a standard Survey, Madame Secretary?" he asked her formally, because this was the reason he'd been recalled to Horwin, no doubt.

"It might be possible to leak any useful findings to your new friends in Amaechi, Knight," she replied. "To give them options, if they did choose to depart *Copez* space for what might be a permanent emigration."

Yeah, he could see that. Survey quality maps that told you where to go, where to avoid, and who might be out there. Save a lot of hassle and effort.

And Toshiko's people would appreciate that.

"I'll do what can, ma'am," he said.

"I expect no less, Maddox," she replied. "You'll have a week or so in the shipyard, getting everything adjusted, then expect orders for your next great adventure."

"Aye, sir," he replied automatically, standing when she did and shaking the hand she held out. "We'll get it done."

Survey Corps.

First In The Field.

ABOUT THE AUTHOR

Blaze Ward writes science fiction in the Alexandria Station universe (Jessica Keller, The Science Officer, First Centurion Kosnett, etc.) as well as The Corsac Fox and several other science fiction universes. He also writes action-thriller (present day as well as historic). In addition, he's the editor and publisher of Boundary Shock Quarterly Magazine and Thrill Ride Magazine. You can find out more at his website www. blazeward.com, as well as Bluesky, Goodreads, and other places.

Blaze's works are available as ebooks, paper, and audio, and can be found at a variety of online vendors (Kobo, Amazon, and others) as well as the Knotted Road Press website directly. His newsletter comes out monthly and you can also follow his blog and his Patreon on his website. He really enjoys interacting with fans, and looks forward to any and all questions—even ones about his books!

Never miss a release!

If you'd like to be notified of new releases, sign up for my newsletter.

http://www.blazeward.com/newsletter/

Buy More!

Did you know that you can buy directly from the KRP website?

https://www.knottedroadpress.com/shop/

Connect with Blaze!

Web: www.blazeward.com
Boundary Shock Quarterly (BSQ):
https://www.boundaryshockquarterly.com/

ABOUT KNOTTED ROAD PRESS

Knotted Road Press publishes dynamic fiction set in exotic locations. Our authors cover a wide range of genres including science fiction, fantasy, mystery, literary, and poetry. We also have unique non-fiction voices in genres such as autobiography, business, cookbooks, and how-tos. We offer both DRM-free ebooks and print books for a global readership.

www.KnottedRoadPress.com